THE HUSBANDS NEXT DOOR

ENJOY!!

K. Moriarty.

THE HUSBANDS NEXT DOOR

Kathy Moriarty

Published by Kathy Moriarty

A CIP catalogue record for this book is available from the British Library.

ISBN 978-0-9932670-0-0

Book layout and cover design by Clare Brayshaw
Cover images © Wetnose1, © Ron Chapple, © Suto Norbert
Dreamstime.com

Prepared and printed by:

York Publishing Services Ltd
64 Hallfield Road
Layerthorpe
York YO31 7ZQ

Tel: 01904 431213

Website: www.yps-publishing.co.uk

To all those people who have
contemplated swapping partners for fun,
let this be a warning to you …

Acknowledgements

Thank you to my darling daughter, for all your help in getting the book published and realising my dream.

Chapter One

'I need you home tonight. We're having a visitor and you'll need to help look after him,' my father told me.

'I'll be there,' I promised.

I was always such a good girl. Well behaved, polite, mannered, I did everything my parents asked of me. That's just how it was when I grew up. You'd never catch me scrumping or playing Knock Down Ginger.

It was a different world back then. Post-war austerity meant that I was conditioned to accept what life offered me without question because that was all that was available. The thought simply never occurred to ask whether it was what I really wanted or if it was right for me. You made do with what you could get and were grateful for it.

I was born in 1940 at the outbreak of the war and things were very difficult, especially living in London. My earliest recollection as a child is sitting under the kitchen table with my mum while the bombs were dropping. We did not have much contact with my dad until 1945 and the war made him a very strict father and I grew up in fear of displeasing him. When my younger sister asked me to say a few words at my mother's 90th birthday recently, I declined because I remember my childhood as being cold, hungry and unhappy and that was not nice to hear.

The eldest of four children, with thirteen years separating me from the youngest, my parents looked to me to take care of the younger ones and I rose to the challenge, just as any dutiful daughter would. I was known as 'the little mother.' My parents made it clear that their word was law and my teen years were spent acting as unpaid nanny to my two younger brothers and sister. I didn't mind too much, although I wouldn't have minded the opportunity to let my hair down a little, but missing out on typical teenage fun meant that boyfriends were out of the question.

I suppose you could say that it was my naïveté that made me ripe for the plucking when I met Robert.

I'll never forget the roar of the motorbike as it pulled up outside our house. There's always something rather exciting about a man on a bike, but since Robert had been engaged and was a fair few years older than I was, I wasn't going to let myself take much notice of him.

My father got up to let him in, and a tall man in waterproof leathers strode in. Striking rather than handsome, Robert was the star pupil at my father's college, where he'd studied brickwork. Having recently passed with honours, he'd come to discuss the arrangements for the presentation following the end of year exams.

'This is Kathy,' my father told him, as I stood up to shake Robert's hand.

'Pleased to meet you,' he smiled, shaking my hand firmly.

I gave him a half-hearted smile, too shy to start a conversation; too socially awkward to know what to say. It didn't take long before he and my father were deep in discussion about the details of the event and I'm afraid to say that after I brought them some tea, I fell asleep on the sofa, bored to tears.

My mother shook me awake what must have been a couple of hours later. 'Robert's leaving now,' she told me.

Robert was standing in the middle of the room, an amused look on his face as I suddenly stood up, still half asleep and disoriented.

'Well? Help him on with his gear,' urged my mother, as I blushed and stepped forward to hold his weatherproof suit for him. I avoided looking in his eyes, keeping my attention firmly focused on his clothing. Years later, Robert told me that it was my apparent disinterest in him that made him curious and want to know more about me. Of course it would. Why wouldn't a woman immediately fall at his feet?

It was a while before I saw him again and, funnily enough, I hadn't spent my time pining over a man I'd exchanged a handful of words with. Since my father was one of Robert's tutors, he was expected to attend the end of year prize giving, and as I'd recently completed a year's secretarial course at the same college, I went along to the event where I happened to be seated at the same table as Robert's parents.

'Mrs Andrews. How lovely to meet you,' my mother said to her. 'Have you met my daughter, Kathy?'

Mrs Andrews and I exchanged pleasantries and the two proud parents did what mothers do best: match make their children. 'Robert's just started work,' Mrs Andrews told us. 'He's being trained as a General Foreman in the building trade. My Robert's really going to make something of his life. He's such an ambitious boy.'

'He'll make some lucky girl a good husband one day,' replied my mother, giving me a knowing look. I rolled my eyes (when she couldn't see me, of course) and tuned out of their conversation. I'd already decided I wasn't interested in Robert and I certainly wasn't going to be drawn into a discussion that might see me committed to a date I didn't want to go on.

All that changed when Robert came to visit my father once more. He found my father with his head buried deep in the engine of my mother's Austen Ruby car, desperately trying to coax some life out of the old girl.

'Can I help?' he offered.

'Well you can't do a worse job than I have,' my father replied, passing his tools over to Robert. 'Be a love, Kathy, and go and get the man a drink.'

I went inside to fetch some juice and when I returned, Robert was busy doing something arcane under the bonnet. My father left him to it and I settled myself down comfortably on the grass verge next to where the car was parked.

'What's the prognosis, doctor?' I asked.

'Well, it's hard to say,' came the muffled reply. 'It could be any number of things.' Robert went on to detail all the potential issues with the car, his mechanical jargon going right over my head. Still, it had to be said that there was something rather pleasant about spending my time in the company of a nice, young gentlemen.

'I don't know if I'll be able to spend too long working on it,' Robert told me. 'I'm supposed to go to the cinema with Jack.'

'Well I'm sure my father will be grateful for whatever you can get done,' I replied. 'What are you going to see?'

'I'm not sure. I think there's a Peter Sellers flick out, but I don't really pay much attention to what's going on. It's just nice to get out, you know?'

'I suppose.'

I sat with Robert all afternoon, holding tools for him and bringing him more tea. I'm not ashamed that I rather enjoyed the view as I watched him in his dirty clothes hard at work. My mother seemed to be happy to let me take some time away from the household chores and having the afternoon free was a rare treat.

'So. How about it then?' Robert said, finally emerging from underneath the bonnet to shut it, the car restored to good health.

'How about what?'

'The movies. Something tells me you'll be better company than Jack.'

My jaw dropped. I couldn't stop the surprise showing on my face. Someone was asking me out on a *date*?

I rushed inside to tell my mother, who laughed at my astonishment.

'He's been trying all afternoon to ask you out, but you didn't take the hint,' she laughed. 'What did you say?'

'What do you mean?'

'Well you did say you'd go, didn't you?'

Oh my goodness! I'd been so stunned by Robert's invitation that I hadn't thought to reply!

I raced back outside again, where Robert was casually leaning against my mother's car, wiping his hands.

'What time do we need to leave?' I smiled.

~

Robert was a perfect gentleman throughout the movie and as we strolled home, he casually took my hand as if we'd been a couple forever. That simple act sent a thrill of excitement through me. Looking back it seems silly now, but Robert was the first man who'd shown any interest in me and now he was happy to walk around in public showing the world that we were together.

As we approached my house, Robert turned to me. 'I want to see you again,' he said. 'How does next Friday sound?'

Rather taken aback, I stumbled over my reply, but I managed to stutter out a yes. Robert smiled and leaned forward to kiss me, a sweet, chaste kiss that was a pleasant surprise. Ever the gentleman, he walked me to my door, bidding my parents good night before reminding me that we'd see each other very soon.

And just like that, I had a boyfriend. Not only that, a boyfriend who made it very clear that he wanted to be a fiancé very soon, with marriage to follow not long after.

His proposal came out of the blue, not long after we'd met. Although we'd discussed marriage, I'd always seen it as something that would happen later rather than sooner. Robert had other ideas, not the first time in our stormy relationship that we'd disagree on major, life changing decisions.

But more about that later.

He asked and I said yes. What girl wouldn't? Robert was good looking, had a stable career, a sensible head on his shoulders, everything that we were told a young lady would want in a suitor. It was all terribly overwhelming and I suppose I got swept up in a fantasy where we would get married and live happily ever after with our 2.4 children and white picket fence, just like all those other happy wives in suburbia.

If I'm honest, there was a large part of me that wanted to get married so I could escape my home. I was tired of being the one that did all the work of keeping the household together and I wasn't what you would call to with my parents. If I was going to do all that hard work, I'd rather it was *my* home and *my* children, and Robert seemed like a good bet to make that happen.

Much as he could be spontaneous and impetuous, Robert also had a more reserved side, which was never more in evidence than when we went away on holiday to a camp in Devon. We were still only courting, and in those days, it was simply not done for an unmarried couple to stay in the same room, so we booked two single chalets.

Still, a girl dreams of what might happen and since we were going to be married, what harm would it do if we enjoyed each other before tying the knot?

Our first day passed uneventfully, the weather warm and pleasant. It was the first time I'd been away from my parents, let alone with a man, and I was revelling in the sense of freedom it gave me. I felt like throwing caution to the wind and after the first night sleeping on my own in my chalet, I knew that I wanted to move.

'Robert,' I began tentatively over breakfast. 'Do you want me to move into your chalet with you?'

Robert dropped his cutlery, looking around furtively to see if anyone had overheard me.

'What do you mean?'

'Well, it's just that here we are, away from anyone who knows us. It seems like the perfect opportunity to get to know each other a little better. After all, you never know. I might snore really badly and then you'd thank me for saving you from making a terrible mistake!'

Robert laughed a little at that, but still hesitated in replying.

'Come on, Robert. Don't you think it would be fun?'

At last, he nodded his head. 'But no monkey business, young lady, do you hear me?'

I giggled, but little was I to know that he meant it.

That night, although the bed was small, Robert did his best to keep a respectable distance between us, the only contact our hands holding each other. 'Aren't you going to kiss me?' I asked in disappointment. Robert leant across and gave me a quick peck on the cheek before retreating back to his side. Unbelievable as it may seem, we shared the same bed for a whole week and didn't once made love, my virginity and good reputation left intact.

At the beginning of the second week, Robert sat up in bed that morning and sighed heavily. 'I'm sorry, Kathy, but I just can't do this any more.'

'Do what?' I asked in alarm, thinking that he was breaking up with me.

'I can't allow you to stay in my chalet, not until we're married. We're betraying our parents' trust by doing this and I respect your parents far too much to do that to them. Besides, imagine what would happen if you fell pregnant? I can't have that and I don't think it's what you want either. You're just going to have to move back to your own room.'

'If you're sure,' I said, feeling utterly rejected.

'I am.'

I didn't argue with him and quickly got dressed and packed, moving back to my chalet as he'd requested. In fact, I never argued with him at all during the entire course of our marriage. Sometimes I think that I should have been more demanding and not so accommodating. Maybe things would have been different then. Of course, Robert was right. It would have been bad if I became pregnant, although not perhaps the end of the world, given our pending marriage. However, it was cruel of him, almost inhuman, to send me back to my chalet feeling undesirable and unlovable.

~

As the weeks progressed, I began to see more of this side of Robert, the handsome charmer gradually being replaced by someone colder, more standoffish in his bearing. It didn't take long before I started to doubt the wisdom of committing myself to marriage so soon after leaving college and starting work. I wanted to see a little of the world before settling down, something it was clear Robert would never consider, take some time to enjoy the freedoms and benefits being an adult brought.

'Mum, can I talk to you?' I asked my mother one afternoon when it was just the two of us at home.

'What's wrong?'

Sitting down with a cup of tea over the kitchen table, I poured my heart out to my mother. I skipped over the details of our holiday away, but I told her how it felt as though Robert viewed me more as a trophy than a living, breathing woman with needs and wants. The more I thought about it, the more I doubted whether he really was the right man for me.

'You're talking to the wrong person,' my mother said when I'd finally finished speaking. 'You need to tell all this to Robert.'

'Oh I couldn't possibly.' I was shocked at the very idea. Robert hated any kind of emotional discussion and quickly changed the subject if it seemed as though I might be upset by it.

'You have to,' she told me coldly. 'It's not fair to string him along, believing that you're going to get married. If he's not the right one for you, then it will be easier in the long run to tell him now before things really get complicated. Would you want to leave him standing at the altar? Not to mention how much it will have cost your father and I to pay for the wedding.'

I had to admit that Mum had a point.

'You think about it some more,' she advised me. 'I'm sure you'll do the right thing. Why don't you wait until after Christmas to talk to him about it? It's only a couple of weeks away and it'll give you time to think about what you want.'

'Thanks, Mum. I will.' As the last few days before Christmas slipped away, I became firm in my resolve to tell Robert that the engagement was off.

Christmas Day dawned and I spent it with my family opening presents around the tree and helping my mother prepare the Christmas lunch. Robert was joining us and when I opened the door to him at one o'clock, I had to admit that he did look very smart in his suit.

'This is for you,' he smiled, passing me a small box wrapped in tissue paper.

I opened it to discover a delicate gold pendant in the shape of a heart. 'This must have cost you a fortune,' I gasped, as Robert placed it around my neck.

'Only the best for my future wife,' came the reply.

In that instant, my resolve melted. It was such a thoughtful gift; so beautiful. How could I be so stupid as to casually walk away from marriage to a good man?

I resolved to commit myself more deeply to our engagement and for a while, it worked. We even booked a holiday for the following September, once more booking two single chalets, this time in Cornwall.

But it was no good. As the weeks wore on and I saw more of Robert, I also saw more of the behaviour that had me questioning whether a relationship between the pair of us could ever work.

I don't know what it was about that Saturday afternoon in spring that gave me the courage to speak up. We were walking along the hop fields where I lived and I had the sudden urge to tell Robert how I'd been feeling for months.

I stopped walking and when he turned to see what was wrong, I said 'I've got something to tell you. The way I feel at the moment, I don't think I am ready for marriage just yet and I don't want to get engaged.'

I don't know what kind of response I was expecting from Robert, but it certainly wasn't what I got.

'Right,' he snapped. 'If that's the way you feel, we'll finish it.'

There was me thinking that we could talk things through, maybe find some reassurance from Robert. I hadn't thought that breaking off our engagement would mean the end of our relationship entirely. I just wanted some more time to think about things.

Struggling to put my thoughts into words, I told him 'I like you very much and I would like to be your girlfriend, but I don't think I can go on under the illusion that we are going to get married if I'm having doubts.'

Robert laughed bitterly. 'No. That's it. We'll finish it.'

We walked back to my house in stony silence. Mutual friends of ours were getting married in six weeks' time and Robert had been asked to be best man. When we reached my door, he mentioned the wedding and asked if I was still willing to go with him.

'Of course I am. I told you. I still want to be your girlfriend.'

Robert shook his head dismissively and turned to walk away. 'I'll see you at the wedding,' he threw over his shoulder.

I'm not sure what he thought his approach was going to achieve. I think he thought that he'd let me stew on my decision and then when I saw him again, having been deprived of his company for six weeks, I'd change my mind and resume our friendship.

I can't deny that when the day came, I did feel a little melancholy. It was tough to see Robert standing by the groom, sitting with the other guests as his partner for the day, but without a ring on my finger or a wedding day on the horizon.

Afterwards, I could see the bride, Barbara, talking to Robert at the reception. She had with her a very attractive friend and from what I could make out, the pair of them were getting on very well together.

I couldn't bear to watch and left the room to get some air. Not long after, I heard footsteps behind me. Turning around, I could see Robert approaching. I wiped my eyes and attempted to tidy up my appearance a little, not wanting him to see how he'd affected me. I was firm in my resolve that now was not the right time to get married, but it was still difficult to see Robert moving on so quickly.

'Nice wedding, wasn't it?' he asked, standing next to me.

'Lovely,' I nodded. 'Barbara looked beautiful.'

'Yes, she did.'

We stood in awkward silence together. It was hard to know what to say. We weren't seeing each other and what was left was hardly what you could describe as a friendship. Besides, neither of us had ever been much good at small talk.

'Look,' began Robert. 'I was wondering whether you'd let me take you home? It seems daft you getting a cab when it's not too far out of my way.'

'No, I'm fine, thank you all the same,' I replied. 'I've already arranged a lift.' I was lying, but I wasn't in the mood for any kind of argument, which would result in my capitulating, as always. If I allowed him to see me home, I'd be giving him false hope that we might get back together again and that wasn't an option.

'All right then. If you're sure.' His tone was curt and he strode back inside, presumably to find Barbara's pretty friend.

~

Robert had left some of his things at my home and the next morning, I made a pile of them in the living room. It seemed inappropriate to keep them since we weren't going to get back together, but I didn't fancy the inevitable confrontation when I took them back.

I sat on the sofa looking at them, wondering what I should do.

'Shall I give you a lift over to Robert's so you can take them back?' came a voice from the door.

I looked over to see my father and I nodded gratefully.

'Come on, then.'

It didn't take long to load Robert's possessions into my father's car and we drove over to his home. Mrs Andrews opened the door.

'Kathy! How lovely to see you,' she smiled. 'But where's Robert? Isn't he with you?'

'I'm sorry,' I told her. 'I haven't seen him since yesterday evening.'

'How strange.' A worried frown furrowed her forehead. 'He didn't come home last night. I thought he was with you.'

'Why would he be?' I asked and then I realised. Robert hadn't told his mother about our split. 'I'm sorry, Mrs Andrews. Robert and I stopped seeing each other a few weeks ago.'

'Oh, my dear. I'm so sorry to hear that,' she said. 'I did wonder why he'd been spending so much time in his room, but I put it down to wedding planning. I hope you're all right?'

'I'm fine, Mrs Andrews,' I assured her. I just wanted to bring over some of Robert's things for him. Can I leave them with you?'

'Of course, of course. Would you like to come in for some tea? Robert should be home soon. It's unusual for him to be out so long without warning.'

I looked at my father, who slightly shook his head.

'Thank you for the offer, Mrs Andrews, but we can't stay,' I told her.

'I understand,' she said sadly, as we went back to my father's car.

~

The summer flew past and I barely had a moment to mourn my new single status, so caught up was I with my new job. I thrived on the work, but the long hours left me tired when I went home at the end of the night and weekends were family time.

One weekend, friends of ours who had a minibus offered to take our family out for a ride for the afternoon. It's strange sometimes the tricks fate plays on us. As we drove around the countryside, we rejected one pub or place after another, not wanting to go anywhere that I might see Robert.

Eventually, we pulled up outside a little pub near Maidstone called the Crown and Anchor. Walking in, we bumped straight into Robert who was there with his new girlfriend, Barbara and her husband and a few other friends. Sure enough, he'd started seeing the girl from the wedding and he looked so smart in his new suit that I found myself immediately regretting my decision to let him go. I later found out that Robert had been saving up for my engagement ring and when I called it off, he'd spent all the money on new clothes.

We exchanged pleasantries, my father moving us along as quickly as possible. Still, the damage was done and little darts of jealousy were worming their way towards my heart. I began to wonder whether I'd done the right thing in rejecting Robert's offer to take me home, so when Barbara suggested that I might like to come and see her next week in her new place, I jumped at the chance, eager for the opportunity to find out the details of Robert's new relationship.

Barbara had moved into a small but pretty two up, two down with her new husband and I could tell that she was loving every minute of playing the housewife.

'Sit down,' she invited, as she bustled off to fetch the tea things. 'I'm so glad we bumped into you the other day,' she went on, pouring out my tea. 'I saw how you looked when you met Robert and I wanted to know if you had any regrets.'

Good old Barbara. I could always rely on her to be blunt and to the point.

'Well, if I'm truly honest, I have to admit that I'm sorry I called it off. I made a mistake and when I saw him with that other girl, I realised that.'

'I *knew* it!' Barbara practically clapped her hands with glee.

'But what does it matter?' I pointed out. 'It's too late now. I've lost him.'

'Don't speak so soon,' Barbara advised. 'A little bird tells me that it might not be going well with Liz. I might be able to put in a good word for you. Once he knows that you're interested, I think he'll come running back, you just mark my words. We're seeing him next week. I'll have a chat and tell him how you feel, if you like.'

'Would you?'

'That's what friends are for!'

However, when I told my mother about her conversation, she had some advice for me. 'Don't leave it to Barbara to say anything. After all, isn't that Liz her friend? I'm sure her heart was in the right place, but you were the one who broke things off, so it's up to you to take the first step towards reconciliation.'

'You're right,' I sighed. 'But it's not as though I can just turn up on his doorstep unannounced, is it? What if Liz is there?'

'Why don't you write to him?'

So that's what I did. I sat down that afternoon and poured my heart out, telling Robert that our time apart had made me reconsider and hoped that he'd still want me. I sealed the envelope with a kiss just for luck and my heart was pounding when I dropped it through the pillar box. What if Robert just laughed when he read it? Even worse, what if he recognised my handwriting and destroyed it without even a glance?

I needn't have worried. As soon as he received the letter, he rang to tell me that he'd like to see me the following Saturday. He wouldn't go into details and I spent the week agitated, convinced that he was coming round to tell me to stop bothering him and let him get on with his new relationship.

By the time Saturday came around, I was a bundle of nerves and I spent the morning watching the hands of the clock creeping around, feeling as though time had stood still.

At last the doorbell rang and I raced to answer.

'And so when do we get married then?' asked Robert without preamble.

'As soon as you like,' I replied.

Chapter Two

I was twenty one when Robert and I were married. Like any young bride, I started married life full of big plans. I was going to be the perfect housewife, the loving mother, everything Robert was looking for in a woman and we'd go skipping off into the sunset together, growing old in a world of sunshine and unicorns.

Of course, real life was nothing like that and it didn't take long before I regretted my decision to go back to him. Marriage was a great disappointment to me. I don't know why I thought things would change once that ring was on my finger. Perhaps I felt that Robert would be able to relax once everything was official, but although we were now free to do whatever we pleased with each other's bodies, Robert showed a decided lack of interest in mine. His general lack of affection during our courtship days continued on into our married life and it left me with a nagging feeling of being unfulfilled. It would not be an understatement to say that the sexual side of our marriage was a great disappointment to me.

After ten years of marriage, I made the momentous decision to have an affair. I had no particular person in mind, nor even any plan about how I was going to find this fantasy lover who was going to sweep me off my feet, but nevertheless, I knew that somehow, some day, I was going to find the passion lacking from my marriage with someone else.

Although we were not unhappy and we certainly never argued, we were hardly love's young dream either. Blissful happiness was an elusive dream. We suffered from a lack of communication, which stemmed in great part from Robert's desire to make decisions about how our relationship would progress and my general tendency to go along with them, even when I disagreed. Still, he hadn't done too badly for us. And to the outside world, we must have seemed like the perfect family.

There was Robert at the head of the household, still good looking with a flourishing career, as well as our two children, John and Sophie. But appearances can be deceptive as we all know and once I'd had that thought, I couldn't shake it. Robert was the only man I'd ever been with and time and again I found my thoughts wondering to what it might be like to feel someone else against me.

The promiscuous 70s were just finding their feet and it seemed almost expected that people would be a little more experimental in the bedroom, so the stage was set for what was to be a very bizarre story indeed, and one which must surely serve as a warning to anyone thinking that an affair would be the answer to their problems.

In the autumn of 1971, we moved to Churchill Avenue after spending six months building our dream bungalow, the cherry on the icing of the cake.

There's so much to do when you move into a new home. Decorating, furnishing and, of course, getting to know your new neighbours and hope that they're people you can at least tolerate even if you don't become close.

One side of our home overlooked an empty plot of land, still waiting for development. On the other lived

Rita and Terry Farmer, a couple slightly younger than us. We first met them while we were building our bungalow. Rita saw me carrying some things inside and came over and introduced herself.

'I wish we could build our own place,' she told me. 'There's so much that I'd change about our home if I had the chance.'

'We're very lucky,' I agreed. She didn't need to know that Robert had, as always, made most of the decisions when it came to the layout of our property.

'Is it difficult to get started?' she asked.

'Robert's in the trade,' I replied, 'so we have lots of contact, which makes life easy.'

'Well, it'll be lovely for our Sharon and Nicola to have someone to play with,' she commented. 'It's always nice to have neighbours with children.'

'I'm sure John and Sophie will be very happy to know that there are two children waiting to be their friends,' I smiled warmly.

'Oi! Rita! Where's my tea?' came a yell from across the fence. I looked over to see Terry scowling at her. Rough and unkempt, he had black, curly hair and to my critical eye, he looked like a gypsy. He worked at the local chemical factory as a fitter and whenever I met him, I always thought that he looked in need of a good wash. He certainly didn't make a good first impression on me.

'I'd better go,' sighed Rita. 'His Lord and Master wants his cuppa.' She looked at me and grinned, a twinkle in her eye and I knew that we were destined to become great friends.

I don't think I'd ever really had a very close female friend as Rita. I felt sorry for her in a way because of the way that Terry treated her. Much as Robert might be distant, he was never cruel in the way Terry was. He would put her down all the time when we were there, ostensibly as a joke, but there was always a sense that he believed what he was saying, at least to a certain extent.

It didn't take long for his 'jokes' to wear thin and after he told Rita one too many times that her skirt was too short and her hair too styled, I vividly remember thinking 'I wouldn't let him treat me like that if I were his wife.'

Maybe it was this sympathy on my part that brought us together and there were many shopping trips where I was a sounding board for her to tell me about Terry's latest transgressions. I did everything I could to help her out, looking after her children sometimes when she was ill. It wasn't all one way, though. She worked at the local employment office and it was thanks to Rita that I found my beloved job as a secretary to the director of a local factory.

Inevitably, I got to know Terry a bit more, the longer I spent with Rita, which proved to be a lifesaver one morning when I couldn't get my car started for work. I jumped when he knocked on the window, so focused was I on trying to figure out how I would reach the office on time.

'Need a hand?' he asked.

I nodded, pulling the knob to open the bonnet, before going around to watch what he was doing. Why, I don't know, since I don't have a clue about engines, so wouldn't know what he was getting up to, but it seemed more polite than sitting in the car, twiddling my thumbs.

'There's your problem,' Terry said, indicating a part of the engine. I pretended to look as though I knew what he was pointing at, nodding and grunting at appropriate times while he launched into an explanation of what had stalled my car. 'Still, it shouldn't give you any more grief.'

'Thank you so much,' I told him gratefully. 'Robert's absolutely useless at anything mechanical. I don't know what I would have done if you hadn't have come past.'

'Well if you have any other problems with her, you just let me know and I'll sort it for you, all right?'

'I will do,' I nodded. An impulse struck me. 'Would you like to come round to ours on Saturday evening? I could cook dinner for you, Rita and the girls as a thank you and we could maybe play a hand or two of cards.'

'I'll see what Rita says,' came the reply, 'but it sounds pretty good to me.'

That card night gradually became a regular feature, thus marking the start of a friendship which turned out to be the biggest mistake of my life and caused me countless years of regret and rivers of tears.

I would be lying if I said that Terry and Rita were perfect neighbours. Terry's expertise with motors meant that he spent all his spare time working on cars and sometimes these eyesores would be parked on the road in front of our house for weeks at a time while he mended them.

The more I saw of them, the more I wondered how on earth a couple who seemed so different could ever have gotten together, let alone marry and have two children. They were like chalk and cheese; Rita well-spoken and sophisticated with Terry very rough and ready. They didn't even seem to like each other all that much at times and it could be quite uncomfortable listening to them bicker all the time.

Still, they were really the only friends we had in the area. For a long time, the only other people we became friendly with were a retired couple who owned a little summer house on the opposite side of the street. They came down from London most weekends in the summer to potter in the garden and relax in the fresh air, away from the hustle and bustle of the city and it was Terry and Rita who introduced us to them.

~

Gradually, we settled into a routine in our new home and started getting ready for our first Christmas at Churchill Avenue, which was memorable for all the wrong reasons.

I don't think I'd ever had a more miserable Christmas up until that point. I'd been looking forward to spending some family time together, but, as usual, Robert kept his distance, working on the house, fixing doors and finding endless building jobs to keep himself busy with throughout the festive period. To make matters worse, John was ill and spent most of the time in bed and we couldn't even cuddle up together in front of the Christmas TV because we couldn't get the TV to work.

I'd asked and asked and asked Robert to sort out the TV aerial, but, typically, he'd ignored me and waited until Christmas Eve to do it, so it was too late to call in a firm to fix it.

'You go inside and open the window. Shout out when the picture looks all right,' he ordered, so I went and did what I was told.

This was long before the days of digital television and aerials were temperamental creatures that needed gentle coaxing if they were to give their best performance. I kept my attention firmly on the screen, suddenly yelling out 'Yes! That's it! No, you lost it!' as Robert tinkered up on the roof to find the best position.

At last, I shouted 'that's it. Leave it right there. The picture's perfect,' and settled down to watch the news. Robert's dishevelled head appeared at the open window and said 'you silly cow. I've fallen off the ladder!' How was

I to know that the best position for the aerial was to leave it hanging suspended down the wall?

As if by magic, it began to snow and soon everything looked Christmassy, even if the atmosphere inside our house was anything but. Our first Christmas in our new home dawned in a flurry of presents and wrapping paper and after lunch, we popped in next door for what was to become the customary Christmas drink.

Surprising as it may seem, it was the first time I'd actually been inside number 8 since we'd first moved in and it was certainly a revelation. As is so often the case in homes of men who fancy themselves a master of DIY, Terry had made a number of structural alterations to the layout of the bungalow but hadn't finished any of the jobs properly, giving the home a feeling of neglect. The carpets were threadbare in places and with two dogs living in the house, the general state of the place stood out in stark contrast to our neat little bungalow at number 10.

'She's a slovenly mare,' Robert whispered to me and although I shushed him, I couldn't help but privately agree with him. If it were my home, I'd never put up with those living conditions.

So there you had it. Two families living next door to one another, polar opposites, but soon to be inextricably tied to each other for years to come. Terry was a fitter, while Robert was a white collar worker, a teacher in the building crafts. Rita swanned about the place like a Duchess, attractive and sure of herself, while I was a plain Jane with very little self-confidence. In spite of this, Rita and I got on very well and in no time at all we became very close friends.

Now we were into the time of the year that I hate the most, that dull and dreary period between Christmas and Easter. It always seems such a depressing period to me, such an anti-climax after the excitement of Christmas and the weather generally turns nasty in the New Year.

Still, there were things to be happy about, nevertheless. I was settling well into my new job, finally getting back into a proper career again after a ten year break to take care of our two children. I loved my job and the sense of independence that it gave me, but at the same time, I always got the sense that Robert would have preferred me to stay chained to the kitchen sink.

I remember when we were first married, Robert turned to me and I'll never forget his exact words. He said 'If I find that we suffer from your absence in the home, working, then you will have to give it up.' No discussion, just his decision.

I soon realised that I'd gone from a household where my father's word was law to one where my husband wanted the same authority, which was a far cry from the equal partnership that I'd envisaged. He wanted to be the sole breadwinner and resented my efforts at making a small financial contribution.

The problem was that I hadn't married Robert for his money, much as I appreciated his providing us with financial stability and a beautiful home. It wasn't enough for me, and try as I might to urge Robert to see things my way, he was perfectly happy with how things were.

'You make love to me as a duty,' I told him one night in bed. 'It wouldn't matter to you if we only made love once a month.'

I don't know what I expected him to do. Argue? Passionately pull me into an embrace? Anything would have been better than the response I got: nothing. He sat there silently, neither denying nor agreeing with me, before rolling over and going to sleep as if he didn't have a care in the world.

Was it any wonder, then, that my thoughts turned to what I might be missing out on if I were to have sex with another man? I was coming into my prime, ripe and ready for an affair. If my husband wouldn't appreciate everything I had to offer, maybe somebody else would.

Chapter Three

One day, one fateful day, a friend of mine at work drew me to one side and passed me a bag.

'Here,' she said, looking around to check that we weren't being watched by anyone. 'Take these. I think you'll find them interesting reading.'

I opened the bag to take a peek inside and gasped at what I could see. From the cover alone, it was clear that these were explicit magazines, and I quickly thanked my friend and scurried back to hide them under my desk until I could get home and read them in private.

That afternoon, while John and Sophie were playing in the garden, I shut myself in my bedroom and started to read. The publications were called *Forum* and were stuffed full of letters and stories about all manner of sexual fantasies, perversions and problems. I had no idea that the realms of the flesh could be so complex and I eagerly read through the advice column and the letters page. These were letters from *real* people seeking willing partners for all sorts of sexual adventures.

It was quite an eye opener to a simple, suburban housewife who'd only ever had one sexual partner in her life, the man she'd been seeing since she was a teenager. I could barely tear myself away to cook the children's dinner and I couldn't wait to show Rita, figuring that she'd find them equally interesting.

I set aside a couple that I'd skimmed through and quickly nipped over to number eight while the children were eating. 'Hey, Rita! I've got a little something for you,' I told her, popping my head round the back door. She dried her hands from the washing up and came over, curious. 'Don't let the children see them and you might want to keep them away from Terry while you're at it,' I advised. 'You don't want to go giving him any ideas!'

Intrigued, Rita quickly hid them away as I'd suggested and it wasn't long before we had to have a chat about them over a cuppa. She was as amazed by what she'd read as I'd been. We were in fits of laughter as we regaled each other with our favourite stories, giggling away like two schoolgirls over some of the letters. We were both amazed by just how promiscuous our society really was.

'Can I tell you something, Kathy?' asked Rita, her usually outgoing demeanour ever so slightly shy.

'Of course,' I replied. 'You know me. I'm not going to judge.'

'All these stories have got me thinking that it would be terribly exciting to have sex with another man. Terry's lovely and all, but he's the only man I've ever been with and I can't help wondering what I'm missing out on.'

'Seriously?' I gasped. 'Me too! I've never talked about it with anyone, but Robert and I waited until after we were married to consummate our relationship and I was far too proper to even consider anyone else. It *would* be interesting to see what it was like with someone else, just the once.'

'Oh well. These are just stories in a magazine. It's not as though they're really true,' Rita sighed.

'Do you think?' I said. 'I thought they were!'

'What – even the one where the policeman walked in on them and decided to join in?'

That was it. We were laughing again and the moment had passed. I'd never talked about my lack of experience with anyone else before and it was a testament to the strength of our friendship that I felt able to confide in Rita such intimate admissions. The fact that she obviously felt the same way brought us even closer together, and thus it was that that the first seeds were sown in our minds. Sex with another partner, something I'd always dismissed as mere fantasy, was becoming a possibility, albeit a remote one.

Don't forget that this was the permissive society, the age of flower power when we chanted *make love, not war*! There were always rumours of wife swapping, parties where couples swapped partners for the evening, picking out car keys from a hat to choose their partner, although I'd passed them off as mere stories, the kind of thing that happens to a friend of a friend, but never to anyone who you actually knew.

This was the setting for our sordid little scenario in which the couples living in numbers 8 and 10 Churchill Avenue would swap partners.

As the weeks wore on, Rita and I often discussed what we'd read and became more and more open about our secret desires until that fateful afternoon when Rita came round.

'Right. I've been thinking, Kathy,' she began with no preamble. 'Let's do it.'

'Do what?'

'Talk to Terry and Robert about what we want to do.'

'Are you serious?' I couldn't believe what I was hearing. 'Robert would go nuts!'

'No, he wouldn't,' Rita assured me. 'It's not as though you're going to tell him that you've got someone all ready and waiting for you in the bedroom.'

I couldn't help but giggle at the thought.

'I just figured that we should sound them out, you know, see what they think about it. After all, what have we got to lose? If they say no, then nothing changes, nobody gets hurt. But if they say yes…' She looked at me shyly. 'Well, if everyone's open about what they're doing, where could there be any harm? We could be living the dream, Kathy!'

I laughed again, but this time, I was a little more nervous. What Rita was saying made sense, but it was always so difficult to talk about these things with Robert. Still, we made an agreement that we'd both bring up the subject with our husbands the next day after dinner when the children were tucked up in bed.

Since they say that the way to a man's heart is through his stomach, I made sure to cook Robert his favourite meal that night in the hope that it might make him a little more receptive to what I had to say.

Once John and Sophie were safely in bed, I brought Robert a cup of tea and sat next to him, anxiously picking at the hem of my skirt while I worked up the courage to talk to him.

'What is it, Kathy?' he asked impatiently. 'There's clearly something wrong, so just spit it out. You haven't scratched the car, have you?'

'No, no, nothing like that,' I assured him. 'It's just… well…'

'Come on, come on.'

'Rita and I have been talking. You see, there were these magazines and…' My voice faltered and I was struck with an idea. I got up and headed off to the bedroom where

I'd hidden my copies of *Forum*, bringing them back and giving them to Robert. He flicked through them, his face inscrutable.

'They just got me thinking,' I told him. 'I was just wondering what it would be like to sleep with another man. Not have an affair, not run off with them. I wouldn't do anything behind your back. I just… well… I wonder sometimes what it would be like to be with someone else.'

'I know what you mean,' came the surprising reply.

'You do?'

'Of course.' Robert laughed. 'You don't think you're the only person to wonder are you?'

I couldn't believe what I was hearing. 'So you're not angry with me?'

'I can't see why I would be.'

~

I couldn't wait to tell Rita the next day about what Robert had said.

'I always said there was more to Robert than meets the eye,' she nodded knowingly.

'What about Terry?' I asked her. 'What did he think?'

'Oh, Terry,' Rita laughed. 'Unsurprisingly, he thinks the idea of sex with another woman is the best thing since sliced bread!'

There was a pause. We looked at each other, both thinking the same thing.

We could just swap husbands.

Chapter Four

The more I thought about it, the more it made sense to sleep with Terry. It might sound strange, given that I didn't like him as a person, but the way I looked at it, going for someone I didn't care for meant that there'd be no emotional attachment and this was just a fantasy, after all. I caught myself daydreaming about him, wondering what it would feel like to have his arms around me, how different it would be to Robert.

Of course, there was someone else I needed to take into consideration in all this. There was no way anything could go ahead if Rita wasn't happy. I didn't want to hurt her. I didn't want to hurt anyone. I just wanted to break out of the rut I was in.

I had no idea how Rita felt about Robert, but I knew she was as unhappy in her marriage as I was. We often confided in each other, Rita telling me about their money troubles. That was the one thing I didn't have to worry about. Robert was very conscientious with his finances and although we might not have been what you would call rich, we were certainly comfortable.

'You're so lucky with Robert,' she said to me one morning over a cuppa. 'He's so polite and considerate. You don't have threatening letters over unpaid bills all the time.'

'True, true,' I nodded. 'He is very dependable. If by dependable, you mean boring.'

Rita laughed. 'Our men are chalk and cheese all right. I don't think you could get more different than Terry and Robert.'

'Imagine if the best of both were combined in one,' I said. 'It would be the perfect man.' We both sighed at the thought. It was all too easy for us to get lost in daydreams. Once the idea of swapping partners, if just for the night, had been introduced, it was impossible to shake and our responsibilities, our *children* and any potential negative consequences were forgotten about.

We were being swept into a mad charade, only this wasn't some parlour game. We were playing with our very lives and the happiness of our children.

'How about if we go on holiday together?' Rita suggested. 'You never know what might happen while we're away. It would be a good opportunity for us all to get to know each other a bit better.' She gave me a knowing look and I blushed. 'Terry and I have a caravan and know all the best sites.'

I thought for a moment. 'I suppose I could ask my mother if we could borrow hers. I'm sure she wouldn't mind. A holiday could be just the thing.'

'What about if we went away for a couple of weeks during the kids' summer holidays?' proposed Rita.

'I'd like that.' I smiled. 'I'll ask Robert tonight.'

Much to my surprise, Robert readily agreed. I had worried that he would have preferred for us to go away by ourselves as a family, but the idea of another couple around to share the childcare appealed to him and we soon settled on the last two weeks in July for our break, near my birthday and just after the children broke up for the school holidays.

Rita and I threw ourselves into preparing for the holiday, planning it down to the tiniest detail. We would spend the first week in Wales before moving up to the Lake District for the second week. I was terribly excited. I'd never been to Wales before, nor had I been caravanning and I couldn't wait to get away.

Rita and Terry were old hands at camping, so we followed their lead and booked a week each at two campsites, leaving us a few months to save up.

All the plotting and scheming offered the perfect opportunity for the four of us to spend more time in each other's company and we went dancing, played cards, watched television together and gradually learned more about each other.

Every time we met up, I found myself watching Terry surreptitiously. He really was the polar opposite to Robert, short and stocky with black hair while Robert was tall and fair. Robert was highly educated while Terry was more physically inclined, working with his hands as a fitter.

Terry was outgoing and obviously demonstrative with his girls. I would watch him interact with them and wish that Robert could be more like that with our two. Robert found it difficult to show any emotion at the best of times.

Rita had told me that Terry could make love at any time of the day or night and was always ready for sex. I found myself watching him, wondering if he was thinking about sex right now and imagining him taking me by the hand and leading me off for some time alone for an hour or two. Much as Rita might complain about Terry, I couldn't help but feel that she had the better end of the deal. Robert always made me feel that making love was nothing but a duty for him and I never felt that he desired me as a woman. I would have been happy to make love more often, but over the years I'd settled for what I could get, what little that was. No wonder I was contemplating an affair.

Once I'd overcome my initial prejudices, I found that Terry was very easy to get on with and the pair of us naturally gravitated towards each other when the four of us were together. He might not have been my ideal man, but there was a definite raw energy and sex appeal about him. I must admit that during those times I didn't take much notice of what the other two were doing and at this point, everything was still theoretical. Rita and I hadn't yet found the right time to mention the subject that we'd discussed, which happened more and more when we were by ourselves.

'Do you think we should tell them?' Rita asked me one afternoon.

'Tell who what?' I asked.

'You know.' She motioned with her head outside where Terry was tinkering with a car engine. 'See if they're interested in a trial run.'

A ball of nervous excitement formed in the pit of my stomach. Until now, all our talk had been just that, but it looked as though I was lucky enough to have found someone who was as interested as I was in finding out whether the grass was greener on the other side. If Rita and I were both happy to swap husbands for a night, or maybe two, how could anything go wrong?

'We'll have to pick our moment carefully,' I cautioned. 'Robert can be a little funny when it comes to talking about intimate matters.'

'Don't worry. I'm sure he'll be fine with the idea,' Rita reassured me, but I wasn't so sure. After all, neither of us could really know what our husbands' reactions would be. I was prepared for sparks to fly and our brilliant plans go up in smoke. Robert really didn't like to talk about our own problems, let alone contemplate the idea of a joint affair, especially one instigated by his wife. After all, it might have been socially acceptable for men to have affairs, for all the freedom of the sixties and seventies, it was still frowned upon for women to enjoy the same benefits.

'Come on, Kathy,' Rita urged. Time's passing and it's not long until our holiday. We'd have the perfect opportunity for some alone time after the children are in bed and nobody would ever know. Let's talk to Robert and Terry about it. Tonight.'

I took a deep breath. 'All right then.' Rita beamed and I grinned back. We were in for the time of our lives.

After Rita had gone to get Terry's tea ready, I started planning how best to approach Robert. I hadn't said anything to Rita, but I had a feeling that Terry would jump at the opportunity. I knew that he was attracted to me. Don't ask me how. Women just know when someone's interested. It was a look here, a casual touch there. It was much harder to tell how Robert felt because of his natural reticence, but I didn't think it diplomatic to tell Rita these thoughts at this stage of the game.

Yes, game. It still felt unreal, something out of a fantasy, a game we were playing, like Happy Families, in which we'd have some fun and then all go home to our old lives after the final dice were thrown. Neither of us had any idea that we were playing a deadly serious game that would have disatrous consequences. To this day, I wonder what we'd have done differently had we realised the impact of our 'little idea'.

I started preparing the tea but it was difficult to focus on what I was doing while I was trying to think of the best way to bring up the subject of wife swapping and Robert grumbled about the fact that I'd burnt his chop. Hardly the best start to the evening.

As if they could sense that something was going on, John and Sophie took ages to settle down and go to bed and by the time they were finally in their rooms for the evening, Robert had got himself caught up with something crucial in the garage. He was probably sorting his spanners by size, but it was clearly vital that it be done *that minute* so by the time he eventually settled down in front of the television with me, I was a bundle of nerves.

'How was your day?' I started.

'Fine.' Robert was as uncommunicative as ever and I could see that I was going to have an uphill struggle.

'Rita and I were looking through some magazines the other day,' I continued.

'Uh-huh.'

He wasn't even listening to me.

At last I did the only thing I could think of to get his attention. I came right out and asked him. 'Have you ever wanted to make love to another woman?'

'Why on earth would you want to know that?'

Here goes I thought, taking my courage in both hands. 'Well, I've been discussing it with Rita and she admits, like me, that she was always wondered what it would be like to make love to another man. In fact, she would like to swap and go with you and I would like to go with Terry.' There. I'd said it. There was no going back now.

I braced myself for the reply.

'Dear God, woman. ***No***! How could you even think such a thing? It's ridiculous. The very idea.' He stared at me in disgust, shaking his head.

He was right of course. All those weeks of discussion, daydreaming and wild brainstorming with Rita dismissed in a flash. Robert had brought me back down to earth with a bump.

Good old Robert. I know I could always rely on him to do the right thing.

~

The next morning, I spied Rita leaving for work and signalled to her that we should meet later for coffee. I felt as though everything had become very clear, now that I'd been jolted back to reality and I couldn't wait to find out whether Rita had had the same kind of response.

For the first time in weeks I was able to concentrate at work properly and my boss even commented on how productive I was being. The more I thought about it, the more I realised that Robert was the only sensible one among us and now it was back to the normal daily grind.

All that was left to do was talk to Rita and put the whole silly notion behind us once and for all.

When she rang my doorbell, I prepared myself to break the bad news to her.

She came in, very excited. 'I've wanted to catch up with you all day,' she exclaimed. 'I couldn't believe it. Terry said yes! All we need to do now is arrange a time and a place and we're good to go.'

'Sorry to disappoint you,' I replied. 'But the dream ends here. When I told Robert, his immediate response was to reject the idea flat. And he's right. What were we thinking? It was a beautiful dream, but some things are better just left as a fantasy.'

Rita looked down heartened, but she took it well. 'Oh well. I suppose it was fun while it lasted. Still, there's no harm done, is there? We're still friends and that's all that matters.'

'Absolutely,' I smiled. 'That's never going to change. But I suppose it's all for the best. I should have known that Robert would be the one to see sense.'

'Oh well,' sighed Rita. 'Shall we have a game of cards then?'

~

The next day, there was a knock on my door. I opened it to see Terry standing there.

'Hello, Kathy,' he grinned. 'I've come to fix your car. I've got the day off, so I figured it was a good time to take a look at it, see what's wrong.'

'Oh. Oh yes. Of course. I'll get you the keys.'

Terry didn't come around on his own very often, especially when I was alone in the house and I couldn't help but feel nervous about meeting him knowing what Rita had discussed with him. I certainly hadn't planned on being on my own with him any time soon.

He went out to tinker under the bonnet while I went to make him some coffee. I desperately tried to hide my embarrassment, but my hands shook as I spooned out the sugar and I was consumed by guilt, even though nothing had happened.

I took his cup out to him and left him to it, going back to the kitchen to read a magazine, but I couldn't focus, too nervous about the man outside.

When he came into the kitchen, I jumped, startled by him being so close without Robert or Rita around. 'I've sorted your car,' he told me, washing his hands at the sink. 'It'll do for the moment, but you'll need a new part. I can pick it up at the weekend for you and finish the job then.'

'Thanks, Terry. I appreciate it.'

I stood up to show him out. As we went out on to the porch, he suddenly turned and grabbed hold of me, kissing me full on the lips. Without even thinking about it, I responded and our kiss deepened, neither of us caring if anyone saw.

When we finally separated, Terry looked me deep in the eyes, a meaningful gaze that seemed to say so much without words, then he left without even saying goodbye.

My heart was pounding, my mind in a whirl. That had been my first kiss with another man after ten years of faithful marriage. A passionate, meaningful kiss, one that I could still feel on my lips and would relive in my dreams for days to come.

A kiss that wasn't part of the plan.

I immediately decided that this was one secret I wouldn't be sharing with Rita. It would only hurt her and that was the last thing I wanted to do.

Although I still thought of Terry as a diamond in the rough, I couldn't stop thinking about that wonderful kiss and I knew that I didn't want it to be the last. But what could I do about it? We'd all agreed that swapping was off the menu and I didn't want to go behind my friend's back – nor my husband's.

When Rita popped round for coffee later, there seemed to be something different between us that I didn't think was just my imagination.

'Is everything all right, Rita?' I asked, terrified that Terry had told her what had happened between us.

'Oh, it's Terry.'

I braced myself for tears.

'He's only decided to go on strike, just when we really need the money. That man never thinks of anyone but himself.'

As Rita talked, I couldn't help but feel relieved that my secret was safe. Things felt very strange, our relationship unbalanced. It might have only been one kiss, but now I was keeping secrets from the one person I'd always been able to talk to about anything.

Listening to Rita complain about Terry, I thought about their relationship and how unsuitable they seemed for each other. I'd always got the impression that one of the reasons why she'd married him was to escape from her home and living with her mother. I didn't know much about her life before Terry, but from what little I'd been able to gather, I believed that she'd had an unhappy childhood and had witnessed some terrible scenes between her parents before their eventual divorce when she was a teenager.

Despite her difficult start in life, Rita was always very self-assured with a natural air of grandeur about her. She was one of life's natural hostesses, never lost for words and able to talk to anyone, no matter what their background. She'd met Terry at a party and, after a whirlwind romance, they'd married. It seemed to me that if they'd taken more time to think about it, perhaps things would have been different. He struck me as a most unsuitable partner for her.

~

As promised, Terry came back at the weekend to finish working on my car. Robert helped him and to all outward appearances, everything seemed normal. However, Terry would keep glancing in my direction and whenever our eyes met, I felt as if sparks were flying between us. Things would never be the same again and if it were down to Terry, we would have gone through with our swap by now. As it stood, Robert was firm in his resolve and the subject was never mentioned again.

That would have been the end of things and there would be no story to tell had something strange not happened. Roughly two weeks later, Robert came home from work as usual. The children were doing their homework in their bedroom and there was no one around to hear him when he came up to me and told me 'I've been thinking about what you said and I would like to try it after all.'

At first, I had no idea what he was talking about. What *had* I said??

'The swap,' he clarified. 'I think it would be a good idea if you slept with Terry and I spent the night with Rita. I've been thinking about it ever since you suggested it and the more I think about it, the more it makes sense. We have become a little set in our ways. This could be just the thing we need.'

I couldn't help but be surprised. Robert. *My* Robert. Sensible Robert agreeing to our making love to someone else!

'I'll speak to Rita and see what she thinks,' I told him. What else could I say?

Chapter Five

Ever since Terry had kissed me, I'd wanted to take it further and I felt cheated that there was no possibility of it happening. Now that Robert had given the go ahead, everything was different. In my heart, I knew what Terry would say. The question was whether Rita would still be interested after Robert's rejection.

I couldn't believe it when Rita was as enthusiastic as ever. Now we weren't just planning for our holiday; we were planning our affairs.

Looking back, it seems unbelievable that we would actually agree to such a mad scheme, but agree we did and all that was left was to sort out the practical details. As is so often the way, it was left to us women to arrange everything and we agreed that the best plan would be for us each to have a day out with the other's partner while we were on holiday so that there was no chance of any of our neighbours finding out our little secret.

We agreed a very specific set of rules, the most important being that no one would speak to his or her partner about what had happened on their day out. After all, we were dealing with real life now and nobody could predict how things would go. Perhaps nothing would happen. Perhaps we would have an incredible sexual experience we'd treasure for the rest of our days. Or perhaps it would be a terrible disappointment and best forgotten about. Whatever, it was not something to talk about. It was to be a one off, an experiment, and one we'd not repeat when we came home.

We also decided that Rita and Robert would go first, with Terry and me taking our day later. When each couple had their day out, they were to leave early before the children got up, so the children wouldn't think anything strange was happening, and then they were to come back late after tea time, so hopefully the children would be snugly tucked into their bunks.

With a good couple of months still to go before our holiday, as we started planning our break in earnest, all embarrassment melted away and it became just as natural to plan the mechanics of making love to someone else's husband as it was to map out our routes or put together a shopping list.

As time wore on, it made more sense to let each couple have more than just one measly day together and the swap was extended to include a night together as well. After all, it wouldn't matter to the children whether we came back just after they went to bed or just before they got up in the morning. They wouldn't know any different and we all wanted as much time to consummate our fantasy as possible.

All that remained was to book overnight accommodation for the new couples. Terry and I went for a very exclusive hotel in the Lake District, while Rita picked a Welsh seaside hotel, not far from our campsite in Wales. As the summer drew closer, Rita and I were both in agreement. This was going to be the best holiday ever.

What strikes me now is that I never felt the slightest tinge of jealousy about the fact that my husband was about to spend a day and night with another woman. I was too focused on the fact that I'd finally get to go to bed with Terry and explore another man's body.

By this time, we'd got into the habit of meeting every weekend to play cards, and the more time we spent together, the more relaxed we were in each other's company. Terry's hand would brush over my knee, we'd exchange coy glances, all the while feeling as if we were teenagers at school making our first forays into dating. I couldn't remember when I last felt so alive.

Rita and I were very much the driving force behind the plan. After all, if it were left to Robert and Terry, nothing would ever happen. Neither men were known for their organisational skills. Rita and I would meet up regularly during the week and discuss any new ideas before going back to our husbands to let them know our thoughts. It didn't even occur to me that we were doing anything wrong. Since we'd all made an agreement, that made everything perfectly acceptable and above board, albeit unconventional.

With the holiday still a few weeks away, Rita and I met up for our regular coffee to talk about our holiday preparations. Inevitably, the conversation turned to our favourite topic: the swap.

'I think it's amazing that we can talk about the swap without any jealousy or anger, don't you?' I asked Rita.

'I think it just shows how well suited we all are,' she replied. 'It's going to be a great adventure. I can't wait!'

'Neither can I,' I nodded. 'July seems such a long way away still.'

'It does, doesn't it?' said Rita. 'I don't want to have to wait that long, do you?'

I shook my head and we both looked at each other, thinking the same thing.

At last, Rita put it into words. 'Why don't we have a little trial run?' she suggested. 'After all, you never know what's going to happen while we're away. We might get all shy and then we'll have wasted our one opportunity to have some fun. Why don't we have a night out before then, get the preliminaries over with so we can relax and really enjoy ourselves on our days?'

'I think that's a great idea,' I told her. 'I'll have a chat with Robert and see what we can arrange.'

This time around, Robert was more than happy with the idea and it fell to Rita and I to arrange some time alone for the two new pairs.

We decided that the following Thursday, Robert and Rita would go out somewhere for two or three hours, leaving Terry and me at home to watch the children.

After tea, Robert got washed and changed, ready for his date. I'd never seen him take so much care over his appearance and I was glad for Rita that he was making an effort for her. Things were going to go much better than I had thought.

Robert left with Rita at around eight o'clock and they weren't due back for another three or four hours, leaving Terry and me to have our own fun.

Watching the car lights disappear down the road, the phone rang. It was Terry telling me the coast was clear for me to go round.

Taking the time to check that the children were safely settled down for the night, I raced next door and straight into Terry's open arms.

He pulled me to him and into the lounge where we made love as if it were the most natural thing in the world. My body felt alive where he touched me and there was no guilt, no remorse, just pure sexual passion.

I had no idea that sex could feel like this. For me, it was the most wonderful thing in the world, a brand new experience that opened my eyes to what I'd been missing out on all these years. I'd expected him to be all rough and ready, just like his appearance, but instead, Terry was a thoughtful, considerate lover, taking care to put my needs first and wanting to make sure that I enjoyed myself as much as he did.

For the first time in my life, I felt like a truly fulfilled woman.

When we finally broke apart, Terry made me a cup of tea and we sat together watching television, just holding each other quietly, enjoying the tranquil moment of post coital bliss. There were no words. Nothing needed to be said. My evening with Terry had been everything I'd hoped it would be and more.

We heard Terry's younger daughter stirring.

'I'd better go to her,' he said, kissing me before he left. I took that as my cue to go home and wait for Robert while I relived my moments with Terry. If that was what an hour would be with him, what would a whole day and night be like?

My mind wandered back to the early days of my marriage to Robert. We were poor and struggling to scrape together enough money to buy our own home. I fell pregnant during our first year together and it was going to be hard to afford everything the baby needed. At the time, we were living in rented furnished accommodation and I knew that as soon as I stopped working, we would never be able to buy a house, let alone furnish it.

With the pressure of a baby on the way, I convinced Robert that we should buy a simple three bedroomed house in the Medway Towns. We saved every penny we could in the seven months before I stopped work and we moved into our first home two months before John was born.

Almost everything in our home was second hand, including things for the baby, and, to save money, we did our own removal with our little Austin van. Despite being heavily pregnant, Robert made no allowances for my condition and expected me to help with all the heavy lifting to get our things into the house.

We were now living on a very large, new, private housing estate. I found myself filled with fear that when the time came for the baby to be born, the ambulance drivers would not be able to find us. I'd been told by the hospital to ring for an ambulance and wait at home when I went into labour, but I fretted that it would take so long to arrive that we'd never be able to travel the fifteen miles to the hospital before the baby came.

So concerned was I about the ambulance not being able to find us that when I went into labour at 3 a.m. one Sunday morning, I asked Robert to drive me to the hospital himself, stopping and using the public phone box in the shopping arcade on the estate to warn them that we were on the way.

Sitting in the car, trying to breathe my way through contractions, I watched Robert meander over to the phone box, call the hospital and stroll leisurely back.

Putting the car in gear, he said 'you've got to go back home and wait for the ambulance to arrive.'

The journey back was painful and Robert did nothing to take my mind off the agonising contractions. Fortunately, we didn't have long to wait for the ambulance, although when the drivers remarked how lucky they were to have found our house so quickly, I felt validated in worrying about possible delays.

'Would you like a cup of tea?' Robert offered.

The drivers were taken aback. Most first time fathers were flapping about in a state and here was Robert, more concerned about the ambulance drivers' comfort than mine! They looked over at me.

I shrugged. 'Don't mind me.'

I couldn't believe how calm Robert was being about it all. Our first child was about to be born, but for Robert, it might as well have been a new piece of furniture the way he was behaving.

'OK, Mrs Andrews. Are you ready to go to hospital and have this baby?' one of the drivers asked me.

'Yes, please,' I breathed gratefully, accepting their support in waddling out to the ambulance.

'You'd better follow us in your van,' they told Robert. 'We may not be able to take you back home again.'

With that said, they rushed me off so I could get to the hospital in plenty of time. When we arrived, the nurse on duty took me through the usual preliminaries for expectant mothers and looked around for Robert so she could get my suitcase and let him say goodbye. There was no sign of him.

I was still in the early stages and spent the day alone in a hospital ward all Sunday with still no Robert. By evening, I was in established labour but still hadn't progressed enough to be transferred into the delivery room and had to endure visiting time with no visitors. I became more and more anxious that something had happened to Robert, but I later found out that he'd been told that the baby wasn't going to arrive on Sunday evening, so he didn't bother visiting.

I spent Monday in the delivery room, so Robert finally came to the hospital, but with John not expected to make an appearance for a while still, he was told to go home and since fathers were not allowed to be present at the birth in those days, I didn't see him that day.

John finally arrived at ten o'clock on Monday evening and Robert came to see me on Tuesday. The system was set up so that after visiting the new mothers, the fathers would go and see their babies in the nursery on the way out, so when Robert came again on Wednesday, I eagerly asked him 'what did you think of him?'

Expecting to hear comments about how he had his Dad's nose or ears, I was stunned when Robert replied 'I haven't seen him yet.'

He didn't even seen bothered.

'He's two days old and you haven't seen him?!'

'Well I didn't see where the fathers went last night so I went home,' he shrugged.

I was fuming. 'You'd better have seen him before you next visit me or I will *not* be responsible for my actions,' I hissed.

Years later, I told John this story and he couldn't believe how his father had behaved. Given Robert's behaviour, I swore that I would never have another baby, but those were words spoken in the heat of the moment and I eventually changed my mind. I was so glad that I did when my beautiful daughter, Sophie, was born.

She became such a comfort to me through my hard times – and there were many to come.

Robert's lack of ability to be emotional or express feelings were is such contrast to the way Terri lived his life. I couldn't help noticing the stark difference.

Chapter Six

At home after leaving Terry's arms, I went to bed and lay there, wide awake, waiting for Robert to come home. On the one hand, I wanted to know that everything was fine, but on the other, we'd made an agreement not to discuss the details of what happened when we were with our swap and I wasn't interested in hearing about his time with Rita. I was too busy focused on Terry and how he'd made me feel, reliving those moments in my mind's eye.

At last I heard the front door shut and Robert came straight into our room. He sat on the side of the bed and started to take off his shoes and socks.

'So,' he began, 'how did you manage the evening?'

'We're not supposed to be talking about it,' I reminded him. 'You're breaking the rules.'

'I know, I know,' he told me. 'But you don't have to worry. I won't be upset at all, no matter what happened.'

He finished undressing and got into bed beside me.

'So what happened? Did you do it?' he asked.

'I told you. We're not supposed to talk about it. I'm not asking about what happened with Rita, am I?'

'I know, but I want to know what happened with Terry. Just tell me. Did you do it? I won't be cross if you did, but I need to know.'

'Why do you need to know?'

'I just do, all right. Come on. Tell me. Did you do it?'

On and on he went until I was utterly exhausted. *What the heck*, I thought. 'Yes, we did it!' I shouted. 'Are you happy now?'

'I knew you would,' he said angrily, but his anger was not directed at me. 'I can't believe it. Rita and I didn't go through with it in the end.'

'What happened?' I asked, my heart sinking. What would this mean for Terry and me having more time together?

'We went swimming before going on for a drink. We chatted for a bit and on the way home, we found a secluded spot to pull over. We almost went through with it, we really did, but at the last minute, I changed my mind. I just couldn't bring myself to be with her, not yet.'

I couldn't believe what I was hearing. Poor Rita. I could only imagine the kind of state he would have left the poor woman in. However, if that was incredible, it was nothing compared to what he said next.

'I want to make love to you knowing that you've just been with another man. It's a kind of fantasy I've always had,' he confessed.

I didn't know how to respond to that. Anything I could think of saying ran the risk of making things worse, so I went along with his wishes and slept with him. He released all his pent up emotions and collapsed, exhausted by my side, whilst I stared at the ceiling, feeling completely cold and unmoved.

It was at this moment that I knew that we should never have gone through with it. We hadn't even left for our holiday yet and things were going wrong. I could see that there would be tears before long and I was right.

~

Robert left for the work the next morning as if it were any other day. He seemed calm and carefree, as if nothing had happened, even though it was obvious to me that there was disaster looming.

I managed to catch Rita at the garden fence before I had to leave for work.

'How did you get on with Terry?' she asked. 'Did everything go all right?'

Without thinking, I replied 'yes, we made love.'

Immediately the words left my lips I wished that I could take them back. I could see how careless and cruel it was for me to just blurt it out like that, especially since I knew what had happened the night before.

'Oh,' she cried, looking stricken. 'Terry told me that nothing happened with you. He said that he didn't want to be ahead on the 'swapping stakes' so you'd agreed to wait until our holiday.'

'I'm sorry,' I said. 'I shouldn't have said anything.' I thought for a moment. 'Perhaps the best thing to do would be for me and Terry to go out for a drive tonight while you and Robert stay in. That would give us all a chance to talk things through and sort everything out so nobody gets hurt.'

'I knew you'd come up with the perfect solution,' Rita smiled and we agreed to suggest this to the men.

We all agreed that Terry and I would go out for the evening the next day so that Rita and Robert could 'even the score' as it were. We decided that if the light was on in my kitchen when Terry and I returned, it would be safe to go in.

When the time came to go out with Terry, I was glad to escape the tense atmosphere at home. The pressure and emotional strain was already proving too much for me to handle, even at this early stage.

Terry drove me out to a place on the Kent coast, neither of us saying much as we travelled. He pulled up by the strand and we sat in the car, looking over at the lights sparkling on the calm sea. In other circumstances it might have been romantic.

'It's all going wrong, isn't it?' asked Terry, breaking the silence at last.

'It looks that way,' I nodded. 'Why did you lie to Rita like that?'

'I didn't really have a choice,' sighed Terry. 'It was your Robert. He started to make love to her, but just when Rita was ready for him, he changed his mind. She felt awful that he'd rejected her like that. So what else could I do? She asked me if we'd done it and I thought the kindest thing was to tell her a little white lie. I felt sorry for her and it seemed like the kindest thing to do.'

'I understand,' I told him, 'but everything seems to be getting out of hand already. This wasn't what we planned.'

'To be honest with you, Kathy,' Terry said, 'I'm beginning to feel that I've got myself into a situation that I can't handle. It's so much easier to be with you than Rita. She's always criticising me, always thinking that everyone else has it better than she does. She's jealous of you, you know.'

I raised an eyebrow. 'I highly doubt that.'

'I'm telling the truth,' Terry protested. 'I've really enjoyed spending time with you. I want to see more of you.'

I began to feel that Terry was hinting that we should swap permanently. Panicking slightly, I quickly put paid to the notion. 'I will never leave my husband for you or leave my children, so don't even ask.' I never had seriously thought that I could leave Robert for Terry. I still didn't like him all that much as a man. I disapproved of the way that he treated Rita. I might not have been madly in love with my husband – I would never have even contemplated a swap if I were – but we'd been married for eleven years and you didn't throw that aside lightly. We might not have been love's young dream, but we weren't unhappy either.

We pulled up outside my bungalow at around midnight. Seeing the kitchen light was on, Terry and I went in and I quickly set to work making a nightcap for everyone without actually making eye contact with the other couple.

Rita and Terry couldn't leave soon enough for me and I got ready for bed immediately, wanting the day to be over. As Robert climbed under the blankets next to me, he whispered 'we're even now.'

'I don't want to talk about it,' I retorted, taking his words to mean that he'd consummated his friendship with Rita. I had absolutely no interest in hearing any details about their evening and certainly didn't share Robert's fantasy, but fortunately for me, Robert now decided that he approved of our 'don't talk about it' rule. He rolled over and was soon snoring. I followed not long after, falling into a deep sleep through sheer emotional exhaustion.

~

So we had swapped and there was still another six weeks to go before our camping trip, which left all of us questioning what would happen next. I couldn't imagine that Terry and I would be happy to wait that long before getting together again. Although I didn't harbour any romantic feelings for him, sex with him was like a drug and I wanted more. I realised what had been missing from my life all these years and I needed it to feel complete.

On paper, Robert was a wonderful husband and to outsiders, he appeared to be the perfect match for me, but I always felt there was something missing from our sex life. I'd tried over the years to talk to him about how I felt, but I always came up against a brick wall. I never knew how he felt and communication was non-existent in our marriage. Robert simply couldn't deal with emotional problems and thought that if he ignored them, they'd eventually go away.

Just as in so many other ways, Terry was the complete opposite. He started popping into see me after work before Robert came home. Most of the time, his visits were innocent, the pair of us chatting away over endless cups of coffee, but there was one day when we were carried away and made love in the study while the children were outside playing.

Robert was due home at any minute, which just added to the excitement. Indeed, we only just finished in time, scrambling into the dining room, straightening our clothes, just as Robert put his key in the front door.

'What were you and Terry up to earlier?' he asked suspiciously later that evening.

'Oh, not a lot. Just talking about holiday plans,' I replied breezily. Robert seemed to believe my explanation and Terry and I were safe for the time being at least.

You don't have to love someone to enjoy their body and the fact that we might get caught at any moment brought an extra frisson to our encounters. However, there was a part of me that knew that we needed to put a stop to what was happening before someone really did get hurt.

Two weeks before our holiday, Robert agreed to go up north to work for my uncle. He'd be gone for a whole week to make a little extra money and I pleaded with him not to go, telling him that I didn't want to be on my own with the children. The truth was that I knew that things were getting out of hand with Terry and I was way out of my depth. Ignoring my wishes, as always, Robert went anyway, taking John with him, ostensibly to make my life a little easier.

With Robert out of the picture, Terry came round a lot more during the week and I found myself powerless in the face of temptation. He'd make up some story to tell Rita, claiming that he was going out to see friends, before creeping back to my house and come in by the French windows. I'd be waiting for him, a willing slave to desire.

When Terry reminded me that we still needed to get my mother's caravan for the holiday, Rita insisted that we go together. 'Are you sure?' I asked dubiously, wondering why she'd want us to spend more time alone.

'Of course,' Rita replied. 'You need a man to help you with the caravan and Robert's not around. We don't have much time to get things ready for the holiday. It makes sense for Terry to go with you. Go on. I'll look after Sophie for you.'

Against my better judgement, Terry came with me to collect the caravan.

'Mum, Dad. This is my neighbour, Terry,' I introduced him when we arrived at my parents. 'He's come to help me with the caravan while Robert's away.'

I could tell that they were surprised to see me arrive with another man, but they said nothing, shaking Terry's hand in welcome.

Terry really made an effort to get to know them and by the time we left, my parents had warmed to him.

'I thought that went well,' Terry told me as we pulled out of my parent's drive. 'Now, how do you fancy pulling over somewhere?'

There was a twinkle in his eye as he spoke that I never could resist and as soon as we found a suitable spot, we pulled over. We were like two teenagers making love in the back of the car. Terry knew how to make me feel happy, even if it was only fleeting.

Cuddled up together, Terry turned to me and said 'wouldn't it be nice if we could do this all the time?'

I grunted noncommittally.

'I mean it, Kathy,' he said. 'Leave Robert and move in with me. You know it makes sense.'

'I know nothing of the sort,' I retorted, my relaxed mood instantly evaporating. 'I've told you before. I'm not going to leave my husband. It's completely out of the question, so stop asking me. Otherwise this whole thing's off.'

'Oh really?' Terry gave me that look and started caressing me again. It didn't take long before the caravan was rocking once more.

~

'What's the caravan doing here?' asked Robert as he walked through the door, fresh from my uncle's.

'Rita and Terry thought it would be a good idea if I started loading it up for the holiday,' I told him.

'How did you get it down here by yourself?'

'I wasn't by myself. Terry helped me.'

Robert hit the roof. 'What were you doing, going off to your parents with that man?' he yelled. '*I* was supposed to get the caravan. What were you thinking? What will your parents be thinking?'

This was the first time I'd seen Robert show any type of emotion since the whole swapping mess had begun and I didn't know how to deal with it.

'That's it,' he snapped. 'The holiday's off. We'll go away by ourselves. I don't want to spend any more time with those people.'

'But what about Rita?' I protested. 'She'll be really disappointed.'

'I don't care about Rita,' Robert said coldly. 'I care about our marriage and if you do too, you'll see that I'm right.'

As soon as I got a chance to talk to Rita, I broke the news to her and I was right. She was devastated. 'Please, Kathy,' she begged. 'Talk to Robert. If you don't come away with us, we won't have a holiday at all this year. Terry's adamant that we have to go away with you and I really need this break. You have no idea how much.'

Always a soft touch, I sighed. 'I'll try and calm him down. I can't promise anything though.'

What I should have done was stuck to my guns, respected Robert's feelings and call the whole thing off. Events were spiralling out of control and it felt like the other three seemed to look to me to solve our problems when I was just as lost as everyone else.

Later that day, I was due to go to the school open day with Rita, but when I answered the door to her, a worried look was on her face. 'When I told Terry there was a problem with Robert and we might not go away after all, he stormed out of the house. He muttered something about needing time to be alone and think things out. I'm really worried about him. Could you go and find him? He'll listen to you. I'll take the children to the school open day so they don't miss out. Please, Kathy.'

Once again, I found myself giving in to Rita's request. She told me where she thought Terry had gone and sure enough, I found him easily, sitting alone in a quiet, secluded spot in the local park.

'What's all the drama about, Terry?' I asked jovially, settling myself down next to him.

'You know exactly what,' Terry replied. 'I've been looking forward to this holiday for weeks. I thought we all had. And now to find out that Robert's going to be petty and spoil everything, well. It's just too much.'

'Robert just needs a little more time to adjust,' I reassured him. 'I'll talk him round. But you need to be careful not to do or say anything to upset him. He's rather volatile at the moment and we don't want to give him any excuse to call things off for good.'

Terry took my hand. 'I don't know what I'd do without you, Kathy,' he told me. 'You're a good woman.'

'Well, I don't know about that, but I do know that we just need to be a little more aware of Robert. He is my husband and deserves respect for that.'

'You're right,' nodded Terry, although the kiss that he treated me to gave the lie to his words.

'I'd better go,' I said, breaking away. 'Robert thinks I'm at the school open day and if I'm gone too long, the children will wonder where I've got to. Everything will be fine. Trust me.'

'I do,' Terry smiled.

As I walked back to school, I felt exhausted, the effort of trying to keep everyone happy taking its toll. Quite frankly, by that point, I didn't care whether we went on holiday with Rita and Terry or not.

~

The next few days were a whirlwind of packing and final preparations for our two week break. The children were all very excited and it was hard not to be caught up in their emotions.

I realised that in the weeks since we'd first started discussing the swap, I'd never thought about how it might affect the children. There were four children between the two families and my son, John, was the only child old enough to sense that something was going on, being eleven years old at the time.

Fortunately, he never asked any questions about Terry and my suspicious activity and I was grateful for the fact that he was just like the other boys his age, preferring to spend time outdoors playing instead of watching what his mother was up to.

I was not close to my son. Despite the circumstances of his birth, he had always been a Daddy's boy. Still, he was well behaved and never gave me any trouble, so I am ashamed to say that his feelings were the last thing on my mind. It was hard to tell what he was thinking. He was like his father and found it difficult to talk about his emotions.

The girls were younger and unaware that anything untoward was going on. Soon events would take a dramatic twist that meant that we wouldn't be able to hide our affairs, not from our daughters, nor from anyone else.

Chapter Seven

There are some holidays that are, quite literally, life changing. Perhaps they open your eyes to new horizons; perhaps you meet someone important. Our little camping trip fell into that category and the effects of what went on are still felt today.

We left early on a Saturday morning, the day before I turned thirty two. When I locked the door to my little bungalow behind me, I had no idea that it would be for the last time. I went away on holiday with one husband and came back with another to move in next door, a situation that seems incredible to think about but is nevertheless true.

We set ourselves a modest target for travelling the first day and by late afternoon, we found ourselves pulling into a small campsite to spend the night, having travelled roughly half way to Portmaddoc, our final destination. We set up our two caravans next to each other and Rita and I started preparing our first evening meal as a group.

This was all new to me, as I'd never been on a caravan holiday before, and I enjoyed the novelty of it all. Even washing up seems to be more fun when you're camping!

Everything went well, the children cleaned their plates and I began to relax a little. For that brief moment, I truly believed that everything would go well and we would have a holiday we could all look back on for years to come as our one little foray into wife swapping.

We all had an early night, ready for the final leg of the journey the following morning, my birthday. Although for some people, birthdays are a cause for celebration, Robert never really bothered making a fuss of me on my special day and this was no exception. It was a day pretty much like any other. I cooked a simple meal and we opened a bottle of wine to share together and that was how we marked the occasion.

The weather was gloriously hot and our first two days passed in a blissful haze of swimming and playing on the beach with the children. A family holiday just like anyone else's.

However, when Robert and I went to bed on Tuesday night, Robert turned to me with tears in his eyes.

'I don't want to go tomorrow,' he told me.

'What do you mean?' I asked. He and Rita were due to leave early in the morning for their day out and it was a little late to be changing his mind now.

'It's not what I want, Kathy,' he said. 'Can't we just go home and forget all about it? This all seems so wrong. What on earth were we thinking?'

I didn't know what to say. In that moment, I held in my hands an incredible power over four people's lives, eight if you included the children. All it would have taken would have been one word and I could have stopped everything there and then.

The problem was that I desperately wanted my day out with Terry. It might have been selfish of me, but in that moment, I had no compassion for Robert and wanted to put my needs first, just for once. I could have packed everything up and gone home with my husband there and then, but I chose not to. Going home would have meant that Robert would have got his way yet again and my life would carry on as it always had, but with even less emotion and passion, if that were possible.

And so it was that Robert and Rita got up early on Wednesday morning before the children were awake and left to spend the day and night together, arriving back before breakfast the next day so as not to cause too much disruption for the children.

It felt very strange watching them drive away together. When the children asked where they'd gone, we told them that we were going to have to leave our campsite and Robert and Rita had gone off to find another place for us to stay.

I was not looking forward to looking after four children all day, so we did our best to keep everyone busy so the time would fly past. After breakfast, we set off to explore the sights of Portmaddoc. We went on the Festiniog Railway, which we all enjoyed, and soon enough, it was bedtime. I was absolutely exhausted by the time the children were settled down and glad of the opportunity to spend time with Terry.

Alone at last, Terry and I fell into each other's arms and took our just reward for a hard day's work. Terry's stamina was incredible, making love to me two or three times, the first time in my life I'd ever had such an experience. He begged me to stay the whole night with him, but I refused. I didn't want to take the chance of the children waking up and finding us like that.

I woke up early, ready to greet Robert and Rita on their return. We'd agreed that they'd be back in time for breakfast, but by mid-morning there was still no sign of them and we started to worry. Had something happened to them? Should we start contacting the local hospitals to see if there'd been an accident?

The children were upset and wanting to know where Robert and Rita were, while Terry was fuming. I had no idea what to do for the best, so we all went for a walk up the mountainside at the back of the camp where we had a good view of the campsite. We sat and waited for the lovers to return.

Suddenly we saw Robert's big, green Vauxhall drive up to our caravan. We raced down to meet them and Robert was already hitching up the caravan, clearly in a foul mood. He barely said a word to me as he jumped in the car and I quickly gathered the children together. We set off up the mountain road leading away from the camp, following Terry and Rita, and I finally asked Robert why they were so late back.

'We were held up in traffic,' he grunted.

As we made our way up the mountainside, we watched in horror as Terry drove like a madman, the caravan swaying from side to side, threatening to topple over.

'Slow down, Robert,' I gasped. 'All the time you're trying to keep up with him is just making him go faster and faster.'

After a few miles, Robert realised he couldn't keep up with Terry's pace and I heaved a sigh of relief as his caravan disappeared into the distance and out of view.

Not long after, we saw them pulled in at the side of the road and we pulled in behind them. Terry was absolutely fuming.

'Robert!' he yelled. 'Can Kathy come in with me? Rita's absolutely useless with the maps and it's doing my head in.'

Rita pulled me to one side. 'Please drive with Terry and calm him down before he kills us all,' she pleaded.

None of us wanted to argue with Terry the mood he was in, so I dutifully climbed in with him and we set off again.

'Do you know what your husband did?' seethed Terry.

'No.'

'So you don't know why they were late back?'

'Robert said they got stuck in traffic.'

'Ha!' Terry laughed bitterly. 'That man's such a liar. He told Rita that there was no reason to bother getting back on time and we should just wait for him.'

I wasn't surprised to hear this. Robert was never very punctual, no matter how important the occasion. Just look at what happened when John was born. Terry and I had spent the whole morning fretting about them for no reason.

It was a long way to go to reach our second campsite by Thursday night and with our late start, it was unlikely that we'd be able to make it in time now. Still, the children were getting hungry, so we found a pub in a little village in Cheshire and stopped for lunch at around half past one. Sandwiches and drinks all round did the trick and after a quick trip to the bathroom, we were ready to go again.

Once more, I got in the car with Terry, who was still cross with Robert. Ten minutes later, we hit some road works with temporary traffic lights for single lane traffic. Terry and I made it through, but Robert and Rita were caught by the red light. Terry looked into his rear view mirror and commented on the fact that Robert had got out of the car for a comfort stop at the side of the road.

Instinctively, I knew something was wrong. Robert had been to the toilet with the rest of us only moments before, but we carried on driving. I kept looking behind to see if they had caught up with us, but there was no sign of them until Terry pulled into a petrol station to fill up his car. I went over to the roadside to watch out for Robert and Rita, ready to wave them down if they drove past.

While I was waiting, a car drew up behind us at the pumps. 'Are you looking for the chap with the caravan back at the lights?' the driver called over.

'Yes.'

'Well you might want to get back there. He's just been taken ill at the road works.'

I raced over to Terry, who was paying for the petrol. 'I told you something was wrong,' I gasped. 'We've got to go back. Robert's ill.'

We pulled out of the garage and raced back to the road works, arriving just in time to see Robert being stretchered into a waiting ambulance. Rita was in floods of tears and so were the children.

One of the workmen had managed to take the caravan off the road so the traffic could get going and they'd radioed for the ambulance, who was taking Robert to the hospital, which was just around the corner. It was utter chaos and I added to it when I got out of the car Terry was driving and climbed into the ambulance to go with Robert. I could see the workmen exchanging a few glances, as if to say to each other 'hello. What's going on here then?'

It was only a few minutes before Robert was admitted into the little cottage hospital and I sat in the waiting room, trembling. In those short moments I felt terribly alone and more than a little frightened. My world was crumbling around me. Why on earth had we agreed to this ridiculous idea in the first place? Why hadn't I just gone home with Robert on Tuesday when he'd begged me?

Terry arrived and told me that he and Rita had managed to park the cars and caravans in the hospital car park. He stayed in the waiting room while I was shown into the ward to visit my husband for a few minutes. He was too exhausted to cope with longer.

I was shocked at what I saw. Robert looked terribly sorry for himself and was lying there, almost lifeless.

'Don't worry, Mrs Andrews,' the doctor told me, seeing how upset I was. 'Our initial tests say that nothing's seriously wrong, but we'll keep him overnight for observation, just in case.'

'Thank you.' A horrible thought struck me. Where could we spend the night while Robert was in hospital? We could hardly stay in the car park. 'Do you know of any campsites we could stay in tonight?'

'I'm sorry. I can't think of any.' The doctor paused. 'There is a pub just up the road with a large car park. I'm sure if you explain your situation to the landlord, he'll be able to help.'

'Thank you so much,' I said and went back to where Terry and Rita were waiting for news. The look of relief on Rita's face spoke volumes and even Terry had lost some of his anger. We went back to our cars and found the pub without any trouble. Luckily, the landlord was as lovely as the doctor had said and told us that we were welcome to stay for as long as we needed.

Terry popped out to do a little shopping for dinner and I prepared lamb chops for everyone. Poor Rita collapsed under the strain of it all and retired to bed.

'Are you all right, Kathy?' Terry asked in concern.

I nodded miserably.

'Look, I'll take you up to the hospital for the evening visit. The children will be fine with Rita.'

No matter what had happened between us in the past, Robert was my husband. I thought he'd be my husband for life, so I did what any dutiful wife did. I went to see him, little realising that my marriage was slowly unravelling, piece by painful piece.

Chapter Eight

Visiting hours began at seven thirty and I arrived promptly. Before I could go in to see Robert, however, the sister took me to one side. Nervously, I sat in her office, hoping that there wasn't something seriously wrong with Robert.

'I understand from your husband that another woman is involved,' she began without any preamble.

'That's right,' I confirmed, wondering what this had to do with anything. 'In fact, there's another woman *and* another man involved.'

'I thought it might be something like that,' she nodded. 'We get quite a few cases like this during the summer. You'd be surprised.'

I certainly would *be surprised, way out in the country in a little cottage hospital like this* I thought.

'We always find in cases like this that there is always one person in the group who cannot take the strain of the affair,' she went on, 'and I'm afraid your husband is the one in this case.'

'What exactly is wrong with him?' I asked.

'We're pretty certain it's a combination of sunstroke and stress. Nothing too serious, but he does need to rest. I think it would be best if you only stay for half an hour tonight as he really is very tired.'

'That's fine,' I agreed. I was very tired myself with all the drama of the past couple of days.

I went into see Robert, who was lying on the bed, looking very washed out. He appeared to be sedated and wasn't capable of much in the way of conversation, which was a relief, since I had no idea what to say to him. He muttered something about a pain in his chest, which sent a shiver down my spine, which I'm sure is exactly what he wanted. He hoped that I'd think he'd had a heart attack, but after my conversations with the medics, I knew this was unlikely or they'd have told me.

Still, upsetting as it was to see him lying there, looking so pathetic, I wasn't as distraught as you might expect a devoted wife to be in these circumstances.

'Let's just go home,' he suggested. 'There's no point in finishing the holiday now.'

'Let's not many any hasty decisions,' I replied, patting his hand. 'Let's just get you well again and then we can decide what to do.'

I stayed for a few more minutes and then kissed him lightly on the cheek to say goodbye before leaving.

Terry was waiting for me outside.

'How is he?' he asked.

'He'll be all right,' I replied. 'I'm pretty certain he'll be out tomorrow. They said they think he has sunstroke. For some reason, he told them all about the swap and apparently they're used to these kind of emergencies. Apparently, they get them all the time during the summer.'

Terry raised his eyebrows.

'Anyway, Robert wants to go home,' I told him.

'What did you say to that?'

'I said we'd discuss it tomorrow when he's feeling better.'

'Typical.' Terry shook his head in disgust. 'He's had his day out but doesn't want you to have yours. Well he can think again. We're going to have our day out, you know.'

'Whatever,' I sighed. 'I'm too tired to discuss it any further right now.'

'Come on. Let's go for a drink.'

We went back to the pub and had a quiet nightcap in the bar before heading back to the caravans.

'You can sleep in our caravan if it'll make you feel better,' Terry offered.

I looked at him scornfully. 'Absolutely not. There's no way I'd leave my children alone in the caravan.'

Alone at last, I sank into my bunk, totally spent. Finally, the tears came and once they started, I couldn't stop. I cried half the night. It was the first time since the start of the whole bizarre business that I had sobbed like this. The reality of what we were doing had hit home at last and I could see how out of control my life had become.

I knew the sensible thing to do would be to collect Robert from the hospital and go home as he'd requested. We could put an end to it all now. Yet, somehow I knew this wouldn't happen. I really wanted to have my day and night with Terry, despite everything. 'Yes, have your time with Terry,' I told myself. 'You've earned your day out and you deserve to have something for you, just this once.'

The truth was there was no passion in my marriage to Robert and once the affair was over, it would be back to my humdrum existence. I wanted this one opportunity to experience a little excitement, something I could look back on for the rest of my life.

~

The next morning we had a stroke of luck. We found a proper campsite not far from the pub and decided to move there before going to see Robert at midday. It was a tranquil little spot and there were only two other caravans there, giving us plenty of privacy.

On Friday, I felt strong enough to visit the hospital alone and, once more, the sister took me into her little office for a motherly chat before I went into see Robert.

'He's a lot better this morning,' she smiled. 'I'm pleased to tell you that he can go home now that the doctor has given him a final check-up. I just wanted to have a final little word with you before you leave. I have no idea how you feel about him and quite frankly, it's none of my business. However, I strongly advise you to avoid saying anything that might upset him. He's still in a very nervous condition and whatever your intentions are, I urge you to think twice before making any decisions about your future together.'

'Oh you don't have to worry. I have no intention of leaving him and my children,' I assured her.

'I'm glad to hear it,' she nodded. 'He's a good man and I think you'd be foolish to let him go.'

'I know,' I agreed. 'I want to keep my marriage intact, in spite of everything.'

'Good. Well, I think they'll be serving dinner shortly, so perhaps you might want to wait until after that before you leave.'

'I will,' I promised. 'And thank you so much for your help. It's meant a lot.'

I went in to see Robert, who looked much better than he had the day before.

'How are you?' I asked.

'I'm okay,' he replied, not looking at me. 'I think we need to talk.'

'What do you mean?'

This time he looked me straight in the eye. 'We should talk about us and our future together. Do you love me?'

I had no idea what to say to that.

'Do you love me?' he repeated more forcefully. 'I want a straight answer and I want the truth.'

This was a very difficult question to answer, especially given my chat with the sister. I really didn't want to have this conversation right now for both our sakes, but he was so insistent and I didn't want to lie.

'Well, I suppose I don't love you as I should or as I did when we married eleven years ago, but there must be thousands of couples in the same situation. After all, people change over the years.'

I wanted to explain further, but Robert didn't give me a chance.

'That's it, then,' he pronounced. 'We'll finish it. If you don't want to live with me for me, then we'll finish it.'

'Robert, don't be like that. You're being too hasty,' I protested, but at that moment, a nurse brought in his dinner, which he began to eat with great relish.

I sat there in silent amazement, watching him devour his meal. I couldn't believe what was happening to me. Robert had actually just told me our marriage was over and sat there eating his meal as if nothing important had happened.

I was too numb even to cry. 'Please don't do this Robert,' I begged. 'What about John and Sophie? How would they feel if we divorced? It's not fair on them, not fair on any of us.'

'You should have thought about that sooner,' he said coldly. 'Our marriage is over.'

I thought back to the incident in the hop field back when we were courting and knew there would be no changing his mind. It was just like a bad dream, only there would be no waking up from this one.

When he'd finished his food, he got up and dressed and we left, saying goodbye to the sister on the way out.

I drove back to the campsite, where Terry and Rita were waiting for us. Rita immediately began fussing over Robert and, feeling rather superfluous, I left them to it, joining Terry in his caravan. I told him what had happened, how Robert had just ended our marriage without thinking about anyone else. Terry couldn't believe his ears – but he was more concerned about how Rita had just been behaving with Robert.

At that moment, Robert and Rita came in and told us that it would be a good idea if Terry and I had our day out starting this evening, instead of waiting for Saturday morning as planned.

'But you're not well, Robert,' I pointed out. 'You can't cope with the children, not in your condition.'

'We'll be just fine,' Rita reassured me. 'I suggest you go as soon as the children are in bed.'

'Come on, Kathy. Let's get away for a bit,' Terry urged.

By that point, I just wanted to escape the whole sorry mess, so I agreed.

Terry drove me down into the village where I managed to get an appointment at a hairdresser's to have my hair set. There was a forty minute wait, so we went for a coffee. Unfortunately, Terry had parked in a twenty minute only zone and I remember distinctly sitting in the hairdresser's chair watching the traffic warden handing him a parking ticket just before he left. It seemed to sum up everything that was happening right now, how we were going against social conventions and being punished for it.

When Terry came back for me two hours later, he was clearly happy about the prospect of spending time with me. 'Don't feel guilty about leaving,' he told me. 'Robert seemed to make a miraculous recovery while you were out. You deserve someone who makes you feel special and I'm going to make sure that you have the time of your life while you're with me.'

I could only hope that he was right and it would all be worth it.

Chapter Nine

Terry and I left for the Lake District. As we pulled away from the campsite, I felt as if a huge weight were lifted. It was a blessed relief to get away and try to forget all the tensions and upsets of the past few days.

We had a long way to go, since Robert's hospital stay had cut short our journey on Thursday and we'd ended up camping in Cheshire instead of our booked site near Morecambe. We had to travel twice the distance we should have to a Games Fair where Terry had planned to participate in a clay pigeon shooting competition, but Terry was a good driver and we managed to make it in time for breakfast before going into the showground.

We spent a carefree day at the fair, Terry doing quite well in the contest, but I could tell that his mind wasn't really on shooting. There were hordes of people at the event and we decided to leave mid-afternoon to beat the crowds trying to get out at the same time.

After all the recent negativity, it gave me a thrill of excitement to book into our hotel in Lake Windemere as 'Mr and Mrs Smith'. It was a luxurious hotel, a favourite with American tourists. It was incredible to be alone at last in such splendid surroundings.

Our bedroom featured a huge antique bed and we tumbled in as soon as we could get our clothes off. We made love without a care in the world, even though we were sealing our fate. It was pure ecstasy, the best it had ever been between us, despite many incredible stolen moments together. Making love to Terry made me feel like a real woman.

Terry was such a generous lover, he spoilt me for Robert. How could I ever be satisfied with him again, knowing what I was missing out on? I didn't love Robert and never could.

The problem was, I didn't love Terry either and I knew it. It was pure lust I was feeling.

We had a lovely evening meal in a very grand dining room shaped like a big semi-circle with a spectacular view of the lake. I couldn't get over how beautiful our surroundings were. The hotel was completely furnished with antique furniture, quality carpets and expensive curtains. I felt like a film star on an illicit weekend with her leading man.

We strolled in the grounds for a while before going to bed, enjoying each other's company. Then we lay in each other's arms, reliving the events of the past few days. Our time was nearly over and soon it would be morning, when we'd have to return to reality. We made love one last time and fell asleep in each other's arms, sleeping like babes, but not so innocent.

We booked an early breakfast, determined to get back to the camp before the children woke, as was the agreement. With little traffic on the road, we made it back just before nine and were greeted by an exhausted looking Rita, worn out after dealing with the children.

Somehow, we made it through that day, going through the motions of happy families. Robert, always a man of few words, said little to any of us, other than to say that we should all sit down and discuss the future at the first opportunity, as soon as the children were tucked up in bed.

Once the children were down for the night, the four adults sat in Terry's car to talk, Terry and I in the front, Rita and Robert together in the back.

'Rita and I are going to set up home together and we suggest you two do the same,' Robert began.

Terry and I were too stunned to reply at first, although I suspected that Terry liked the sound of this plan.

'We'll keep the children with us, of course,' Robert continued, which brought me back to earth with a bump.

'Oh no,' I protested. 'How could you possibly imagine we'd agree to give up our children?' what I thought, but didn't say, was that Rita was barely capable of looking after her own two. How could they imagine she'd be able to cope with four?

The debate became heated and eventually we agreed on sharing the children so that each parent had a child of their own staying with them. I would keep my beloved Sophie, but felt that John would be best off staying with his father, given the closeness of their bond.

At the time, I couldn't fully comprehend the impact of losing my son. All I thought about was that there might be problems with another man reprimanding my boy, who was fast approaching his teenage years. John was a Daddy's boy and idolised his father. I thought I was doing the right thing by him, even though it broke my heart.

Rita decided to keep her eldest daughter, Sharon, while Terry would have Nicola. Thus, in a mere fifteen minutes, the children were callously shared out between the households.

We also agreed that the two wives would not claim their half of their respective homes. I said that I wanted some of my items, such as my saucepans and washing machine. I have no idea why I focused on my washing machine, but my life was in such a mess, I wasn't thinking straight.

We decided to leave early the next morning to get home together to face the music. Terry's parents were housesitting for him to look after his dog, so that would be our first hurdle. I couldn't imagine what it was going to be like for them, seeing us all back early with a new daughter-in-law to get to know.

We left in convoy and set out on the M1 towards London. Surprisingly, the children accepted the new pairings very well, not really being old enough to fully understand what was happening to their families. Mind, none of us really understood what was going on.

We stopped together at a motorway service station for some food and this was where we parted ways. Terry and I left first, wanting to make it through London before the rush hour. We soon lost sight of the other caravan and decided to push on without waiting.

When we arrived on our street, we drove past numbers 8 and 10 to see if Robert and Rita had somehow overtaken us. With no caravan in sight, we decided to park in an adjacent street and take a moment to compose ourselves before confronting Terry's parents.

Along the side of my bungalow was a public footpath that led to the road we were waiting in. Terry nervously popped up this path a few times to see if the others had returned. At last, he couldn't wait any longer, so he started up the car again and drove us round to number 10. Telling me to wait in the car while he spoke to his parents, it wasn't long before he came out again and welcomed me into our new home.

I walked in to be greeted by Terry's mother, with tears in her eyes.

'It's lovely to meet you, Kathy,' she told me. 'I can't pretend I wouldn't rather it were under different circumstances, but our Terry speaks very highly of you.'

'Thank you, Mrs Farmer,' I replied. 'Shall I go get the kettle on?' I went out to the kitchen to make that great British panacea in times of crisis. Tea makes everything better.

Terry followed me to help, whispering in my ear 'you're all right. She never really liked Rita much anyway.'

The children went outside to play and it was almost as though nothing had changed, even though everything had.

Robert and Rita took their time in getting back and arrived at around eight o'clock, heading straight inside number eight without making any attempt to contact us.

Terry's Mum helped me with preparing the evening meal, and we discussed sleeping arrangements for the night. My new in-laws wanted to leave early the next morning. As understanding as they had been (and more understanding than I could ever have hoped for), I felt it would be easier for them to come to terms with what had happened in the comfort of their own home.

Still, we stayed up late talking, mainly assuring Terry's parents that they wouldn't lose all contact with their elder grandchild, Sharon, my new mother-in-law's biggest worry.

At last, I went into my new kitchen to make us all a nightcap. Automatically, my gaze wandered to my old home and to two small side windows that overlooked the garden. I'd kept glass ornaments in these windows and I realised in shock that they were missing. I realised that my husband was packing up all my belongings ready to get them out of the house, despite the lateness of the hour and how tired he must be from the journey.

'Terry! Look at what Robert's done!' I called.

Terry came to look.

'He's packing all my things up,' I said.

'You're imagining things,' Terry replied. 'They've probably just been knocked over or something.'

I was right though. The next day, first thing after breakfast, Robert knocked on the door to tell me that my things were all parcelled up and ready for collection as soon as possible. I looked at this cold man standing on the doorstep and struggled to imagine how we could have been married for eleven years and have him dismiss that time so easily.

'Your things will be in the garage,' he informed me. 'Rita and I are going to visit her father for a few days. She hasn't seen him for some time and we think that now would be a good opportunity to change that.'

'What about the things Rita needs from here?' I asked.

'Rita doesn't want anything from this place. I trust we can leave it to Terry to sort out Sharon's clothing?'

I nodded and watched them climb into Robert's car, ready for their trip. As soon as they rounded the corner, I rushed next door to see what they'd graciously allowed me to keep.

Waiting for me I found my washing machine, hoover, various kitchen equipment, including the saucepans I'd specifically requested, as well as bundles of Sophie's and my clothes. In all, there were about six or seven bundles tied together with household string. Not much to show for eleven years of marriage.

'Are you all right love?' asked Terry, coming over to help me transport my things.

'I'd have thought that I'd at least be allowed to choose my own possessions,' I sighed.

'Don't worry. Things will work out,' he assured me.

Terry's parents bid farewell and headed off to London, leaving us to sort through all the things. There was no space for my possessions until we'd removed Rita's bits and pieces, so we decided to swap over all the things I'd been left.

We spent the afternoon going to and fro between numbers eight and ten, changing over everything. I wondered what on earth the neighbours must be thinking. It felt as if the eyes of the world were upon us, let alone the neighbours.

The neighbours! That would be our next big challenge, telling our friends and neighbours about the swap. We had the rest of the week still as paid leave before we had to go back to work, though, and there was plenty to do in that time.

I decided to get started with the washing and stripped down the bed after Mr and Mrs Farmer left. When I went to find clean linen for it, to my horror, there wasn't any.

That night, I slept in Terry's bed for the first time between blankets. Sleep isn't really an accurate description; it was beginning to get light when I finally managed to drop off. I spent a few hours lying awake, thinking about the predicament I'd found myself in. It had all happened so quickly; I hadn't had time to really think through all the implications.

Now it seemed a nightmare, something unreal.

Lying there, between the blankets so rough against my skin, Terry snoring away beside me, it came crashing home to me just what it all meant. Rita would now be living in my lovely home, using my things, knowing full well that she'd left a broken home (literally) for me to take over.

As I set about the housekeeping and chores during the next few days, it was becoming more and more obvious just how neglected her home was. Terry thought nothing of using the house as an extended garage, with motor spares in the kitchen, glass and various plumbing equipment under the bed. I'd never really noticed just how bad it was over the months I'd spent getting to know Rita. Although I'd known the housework left a lot to be desired compared to my standards, she was a friend and I'd never cared about how she chose to live her life. Now that I was living in her old home, it was a different matter. I had to use the kitchen and try to keep the place clean, all the harder because they had a dog which I was not used to dealing with.

What a massive change from my neat little bungalow with everything tidy and in its place. This wasn't what I'd wanted at all.

My world seemed to be falling down around my ears and to add to all the confusion, I'd lost a son, my darling little boy, John. How would he manage with his new mother? What must he be thinking of me? Would he think I didn't want him?

Looking back on our discussions, I'd been more concerned about Robert losing his son than thinking about how it would affect me. I hadn't realised what it would all mean. It had all been so surreal when we were talking about it in the car.

But now I was faced with reality and it was nothing like I had expected.

Chapter Ten

So the holiday was over, the swap had become a permanent fixture and I was living at number eight with a new daughter but having lost my son.

I had no one to talk to. Who would understand? My close friend Rita was now happily established in my home with my husband. My mother was away on holiday and wouldn't be due back for another five weeks.

Robert asked that I help him keep the news from his parents for the time being until his father had recovered from an operation. I was happy to support him in this. His parents had always been good to me and all I asked was that he afforded me the same courtesy.

However, when my aunt phoned my old home number to tell me that she'd just become a granny for the first time, Robert answered the phone and it was with great glee that he explained to her exactly why it was that I was unable to take the call. Thus my parents found out second hand about my new situation, the one thing I had hoped to avoid. Why he couldn't have simply told my aunt that I was out and would call her back I don't know.

At last, it was time for me to go to work and although I was glad for the opportunity to escape my new life, at least for a short while, I wasn't looking forward to the first day.

I decided that the best approach was to take drastic action and come straight out with the truth immediately. Of course there was going to be gossip, but if I were up front about it all, then there was less chance of the rumour mill going into overdrive.

When I arrived, I immediately sought out my boss, Frank. 'Could I have a quiet word with you, please?' I asked.

'Of course.' He took me into his office and sat me down. 'What's the problem?'

I took a deep breath. How on earth could you explain what I'd been through?

'Well, you know that I went away with my husband, Robert, and our neighbours, Terry and Rita?'

'Yes. What happened? Didn't you have a good time?'

I laughed bitterly. 'That's one way of putting it. I went away with one husband and came back with a new one!'

'What on earth?' Frank was completely amazed at what he was hearing. 'I mean, I don't understand. What happened?'

'We all talked about it and we decided that it was best for everyone if we switched partners. Permanently.'

Much as I tried to keep a stiff upper lip, my resolve to stay calm and collected soon broke down when Frank responded with nothing but kind words and sympathy.

'I'm so sorry for any disruption my personal life might cause in the office,' I sobbed.

'Oh, don't worry about that,' Frank reassured me. 'I'm sure they'll get bored and find someone else to talk about soon enough. You know what they say. Today's news is tomorrow's chip paper!'

I smiled thinly through my tears. 'Thanks, Frank. I thought it would be best if I just came out and told everyone from the start.'

'I think you're right,' he nodded, following me out into the open plan office.

I worked for an old family business, well over a hundred years old, and the main office was situated on the factory site, where we produced fertilisers and associated products for the agricultural industry. There were about twenty office staff and we all worked together in the office.

I walked into the centre of the room, Frank by my side for reassurance.

'Could I have everyone's attention please?' I called. The room quickly fell silent. 'I just wanted to let you all know that I swapped husbands with my neighbours next door while we were on holiday.' The room was so quiet you could have heard a pin drop! 'I now live with Terry Farmer at number eight Churchill Avenue with my daughter Sophie and Terry's youngest daughter Nicola. My son is with his father at number ten with Rita Farmer as his step-mother. I can't say any more for the moment and really I just want to get on with my work in peace and quiet.'

Having made my big announcement, I retreated back to my office, leaving everyone to talk amongst themselves.

How I managed to focus on my work during that first difficult week I'll never know, but in many ways, my job was my salvation. It was the one constant part of my life. Work still carried on, no matter what happened at home, and keeping busy kept me sane, particularly because my colleagues respected my feelings and didn't ask too many questions.

~

I threw myself into sorting out my new home. Number eight was a world apart from my beloved little house at number ten. Rita's household was, quite literally, a broken home. There were so many jobs started and left undone, so many simple things that needed fixing or finishing.

I immediately made it clear that I would not tolerate cooking in a kitchen strewn with engine spares and engineering bits and pieces, even if Rita had put up with it. I also made him remove all his junk from the bedroom, including from under the bed.

Sorting through my new room, I discovered mounds of dirty washing in the wardrobe and linen cupboard, some of which had been there for ages. I sorted through them all and was forced to throw many of the items away, so poor was their condition. I salvaged as much as I could, washing and keeping them as working clothes for Terry.

I cleaned the house from top to bottom, especially the electric cooker, which needed multiple scrubs to get it pristine. How different it all was from my little palace next door.

Lucky Rita, not having to deal with such anxieties, which became all too evident when I had to go next door to discuss a few outstanding issues with Robert.

I couldn't believe how nervous I felt, standing on the doorstep waiting to enter my own home. Robert ushered me into the kitchen and we sat together at the dining table to discuss that always contentious issue: money.

Before the swap, Robert and I had run a mail order catalogue together and Rita and Terry had been customers of ours. Rita owed about thirty five pounds, as did Robert. There was also the question of my jewellery, my engagement ring and a few other valuable items. Before we went away, Robert had suggested placing these with his bank to keep them safe and I'd foolishly agreed, thinking there'd be no problem in getting them back again.

Sitting me down at the kitchen table, Robert started the discussion. 'I suppose you're keen to get your valuables back?' he asked.

'Yes, please,' I nodded.

'Well, I've given the matter some thought and I'm more than happy to let you have your jewellery back if you'll cancel Rita's debt with the mail order book.'

'But those are my things!' I protested.

'Look, I'm more than happy to pay off my debt,' Robert said, ignoring my outburst, 'but Rita's debt is really Terry's responsibility to pay off and if Terry isn't going to meet his obligations, then I'll have no choice but to turn to other means to pay his debt…'

I knew exactly what he was getting at and although it was Rita's, not Terry's debt, I miserably agreed to Robert's condition.

'Now there's also the question of the business venture I was discussing with your father,' Robert went on. The two men had agreed to go into house building together part time. 'Given the change in our personal circumstances, do you think this will still go ahead?'

'I have absolutely no idea,' I replied calmly. 'I will mention it to him when he returns from holiday in two weeks. I'll do my best, but I can't make any promises.'

'What about our housing situation?' Rita broke in. 'Surely you must be able to see that it's impossible for us to continue living side by side like this?

'Terry and I have thought about this,' I replied carefully.

'And?'

'We're more than willing to put number eight up for sale and move, but due to the condition of the property-' I gave Rita a look that told her exactly what I felt about her contribution to the home '- we have to make certain repairs before we can even consider calling in an estate agent to value the place.'

'Well see that you get them done as quickly as possible,' Robert ordered.

I left as quickly as I could and told Terry what had been discussed. It was clear this would not be our last conversation concerning finances.

~

As time wore on, we gradually told all our friends when we had the opportunity. We were surprised by just how understanding people were, the initial shock on hearing the news soon followed by general acceptance. We'd braced ourselves to be ostracised for the outrageous act of swapping and were delighted to find that Terry's friends accepted me and my friends accepted Terry as my new partner. My close friend Jennifer, who lived just down the road, looked after Sophie for me during the school holidays and was quite happy to do the same for Nicola, treating the two girls as equals.

Gradually, life settled down to some semblance of normality. Our two little girls got on well together, partly because they were so young and not as aware as the older children about what was happening.

I got the impression that things were more troubled next door with the older two. I missed John more than I could have imagined and it broke my heart to see him standing at the garden fence looking totally confused, crying and asking, 'When are you coming home, Mum?' I'll never forget those moments, and it brings a tear to my eyes even now, after all these years. The impact our decisions had on our children can never be underestimated.

When my parents were due back from Spain, I stayed at my sister's the night before so I could speak to them as soon as possible. I took Sophie with me to see them, but advised Terry to stay at home with Nicola this first time.

This would be the biggest test yet and I was terrified of my father's possible reaction.

'Mum, Dad,' I began as we all sat round the kitchen table. 'As you already know, I've swapped husbands with next door and I'm now living with Terry at number eight. I hope you can understand how hard it is for me and support me through this.'

'Well, I always thought being married to Robert must be like being married to a robot,' replied my mother, surprisingly.

'It's your life and we won't interfere,' continued my father. 'Of course we support you in whatever you decide.'

You could have knocked me down with a feather. I'd always thought that Robert was the blue-eyed boy in their opinion and I'd been expecting my father to admonish me, perhaps attempt to persuade me to go back to Robert.

'Robert asked me to ask you about the house building project,' I told him. 'I think he would like to go ahead with it.'

'Hmmm.' My father frowned. 'I think it might be better to defer the project for the time being, give the dust time to settle. Would you mind letting Robert know for me?'

'Of course not.'

~

Back home, I took the first opportunity available to break the bad news to Robert. He was alone in the house when I called round and he showed me into our bedroom for a little chat.

'Well? How did it go?' Robert was uncharacteristically excited.

'I'm sorry to be the bearer of bad tidings, but Dad feels that given our current situation, it would be better to leave it for now.'

'What?' Robert's manner changed immediately. 'How could he say that? Why didn't he try to talk some sense into you? I would have thought he of all people would have seen how ridiculous this all is.'

I watched Robert rant and rave, biting my tongue. If Robert had wanted my Dad to persuade me to go back to him, he should have asked me himself. I would have been quite happy to go back to my own home and reunite our family, try to forget the whole swap had ever happened.

'Well, I'll tell you this, Kathy. I don't intend to live next door to you for the rest of my life and I certainly don't intend to sell my bungalow.'

Our bungalow, I thought, but didn't say.

'You'd better get things moving and sell Terry's house,' he demanded.

Hearing Terry's name mentioned, Rita came into the room. 'How's the sale going?' she asked politely.

'We're doing our best,' I told her, 'but the estate agents say that we need to carry out a few repairs before it can go on the market.'

'Oh come on, Kathy,' Rita protested. 'You're just being awkward. It's not a bad buy at ten and a half thousand pounds.'

'The agent tells us we'll be lucky to get ten thousand for it – and that's *after* we've spent the money getting it ready. Money we haven't got at the moment, as I'm sure you realise, *Rita*.'

The pair of them stood over me, going on and on, until eventually I yelled at them 'we're trying to sell it as soon as possible. That's all I'm going to say on the subject and I think I'd better go now, if you don't mind.'

Back at number eight, Terry was full of advice about what I should have said to Robert and Rita, but he'd never have had the courage to say those things himself. To his credit, he did start on some of the jobs that needed completing and we struck lucky when a friend found a second-hand up and over garage door which made a massive difference to the appearance of the front of the property. It wasn't long before we were able to put the house up for sale and look to the future.

One of the many ways in which I found myself disadvantaged by moving in with Terry was my new financial situation. In all the years I'd been married to Robert, we never once got into debt or owed money to anyone. Robert refused to buy anything on hire purchase, so we'd scrimped and saved over the years to put together the beautiful home Rita had just walked into.

Not so in the Farmer household. To my horror, we received a summons for money owing on two counts, one for rates and the other for non-payment of a loan. This was on top of other bills that needed to be paid.

This was so far removed from my way of doing things that I really struggled to cope at first. I sat Terry down to go through everything and it soon became clear that he'd left everything to Rita, who had no financial sense whatsoever.

How convenient I thought. *How nice for Rita to be able to just walk away from it all.*

She would have known the dire financial straits they were in before we left. No wonder she was so eager to get her hands on my husband. I had no idea their life was in such a mess when we embarked upon our little adventure.

There was certainly a lot of sorting out to be done. Somehow, I found the money to get the girls properly kitted out for starting school and they looked terribly smart for their first day.

Rita saw the girls leaving for school. 'Doesn't Nicola look lovely?' she commented.

Yes, I thought. *She certainly looks smarter than when I first knew you all.*

I'd always thought that Nicola was a real orphan Annie when I first met the Farmers. She was a very loving child, a bit of a tomboy, but very open with her affections and easy to like. When I first took her under my wing as her stepmother, I told her that she could call me Kathy if she wanted, but she soon accepted me as her mother and called me Mum quite voluntarily.

Any neighbours watching must have thought we looked very strange every weekday morning. First Terry would leave early for his shifts. Then Robert would depart and I'd see him go most mornings. Then Rita and I would leave at about the same time to take our respective children to school. Luckily, the two households went to different schools so we were saved the embarrassment of the school run together and in any case, we were always tolerably polite to each other for the sake of the children.

There were times when it was hard to bite my lip, however.

Chapter Eleven

Two months after our return from that fateful holiday, the couple next door told us that they'd been to see a solicitor and would be starting divorce proceedings as soon as possible. They advised us that their solicitor had told them it would be in our best interests to do the same.

We asked around and settled on the solicitor who acted on behalf of the company where I worked, who came highly recommended.

Terry and I both booked time off work for our appointment with him and we sat in the waiting room, nervously holding hands. As we were called into his office, I felt more than a little trepidation. How would he judge us? Would he think that we deserved everything we got?

'Good afternoon Mr Farmer, Mrs Andrews,' he greeted with a smile. 'Why don't you tell me what happened to bring you here?'

Terry and I looked at each other and I started telling him the whole sorry saga. He listened impassively and when I'd finished, took a moment to think everything through.

'All right,' he finally said. 'There are a number of options available to you, but I think the best way to proceed would be for the two husbands to divorce the two wives, citing the other husbands as co-respondents. If this is agreeable to you, I'll get in touch with their solicitor and start the ball rolling.'

'That sounds fine by me,' Terry replied.

'Me too,' I agreed.

The solicitor made a few notes before speaking again. 'I feel it only fair to warn you that it won't be easy to obtain a divorce under these circumstances.'

'Really?' I couldn't believe my ears.

'Under English law, the quickest way to obtain a divorce is for adultery. However, although it's clear that this is what's occurred in this case, the judge must be absolutely convinced that the adultery committed by one partner is so completely abhorrent to the other that he or she can no longer tolerate the marriage, which is why they're seeking a divorce. Therefore, it is entirely possible that the judge will ask himself why one husband will agree to his wife committing adultery with another man one day only to turn around afterwards and say that he wants a divorce for exactly that reason.

'We need to be very careful with this case and even then, I'm not sure you'll get your divorce at the end of it.'

My heart sank. I couldn't bear the notion of being married to Robert for a minute longer than necessary.

'Another problem will be the children,' the solicitor continued. 'The courts don't like splitting up siblings and I don't think they'll allow the arrangement to stand as it currently is with one child staying with each parent. I suggest that each husband apply for custody of his own children, giving 'care and control' to each wife. That way, the wife in each case could always apply to the children's father for the maintenance of the children. In other words, if the husband is awarded custody, he is legally responsible for the wellbeing and maintenance of the child.'

This sounded the best solution to me and I immediately agreed to this arrangement on behalf of John and Sophie.

There was a mountain of paperwork to go through to apply for Legal Aid and we paid the nominal fifty pound fee for the consultation, before leaving the office. A mix of emotions ran through me. On the one hand, telling our solicitor the sordid details of our case hadn't been the ordeal we'd feared it might be, but the problems surrounding obtaining our divorce and arranging appropriate care for the children worried me. There was always the possibility that all the children would be awarded to one couple and the thought terrified me. Losing both my children would have been unthinkable. It had been hard enough dealing with the loss of John; I couldn't cope without Sophie. On the other hand, the thought of caring for four children all by myself was appalling.

Nevertheless, come what may, the legal wheels had been set in motion and our lives would be sorted out for us one way or another, this year or the next. There was always the possibility that the judge would decide we'd have to obtain our divorce on the grounds of separation rather than adultery, which would mean a longer wait.

Still, the knowledge that we would be divorced eventually made things a little more bearable and we all focused on our lives, Terry and I doing our best to sell number eight as quickly as possible. Robert had been right when he'd said that we couldn't continue living next door to each other, especially once things started getting serious with our respective solicitors.

Even the most amicable of divorces is a nasty business and ours showed every sign of turning ugly. Once solicitors are involved, they seem to take great delight in turning couples against each other, creating more bad feelings than were there originally. Terry and I were doing our best to get number eight ready for sale as but we weren't moving fast enough for Robert and despite telling me that he wouldn't sell or live next door to me, his tune soon changed.

One night, after Terry had left to go in search of the second-hand garage door that would transform number eight, Robert knocked on my door. I'd been quietly painting in the bathroom and after I opened the door to him, he followed me back into the bathroom.

'Are you taking a bath?' he asked hopefully.

'No, I'm not,' I fired back at him. 'I've been painting and just wanted to put the brushes in water to soak now that I've finished for the evening.' I couldn't believe the cheek of the man. He actually thought he could sit and talk to me while I was in the bath!

We made ourselves comfortable in the living room and Robert cut straight to the chase.

'I'm going to sell number ten and I need you to sign the papers,' he demanded.

I was completely taken off guard. 'I thought *we* were going to sell this house so you didn't have to go anywhere.'

'I know, but that was before I realised how long it was going to take you to sell this place. I want to move as soon as possible. If I sell the house now, I want to know if you're prepared to sign the contract.'

I had no idea what to say to this and with Terry out, I had no one to back me up. Robert was asking me to sign away everything before our divorce was finalised and I had enough sense to recognise that this might not be in my best interests, leaving me financially vulnerable.

'I'll sign the papers if you give me a thousand pounds,' I said spontaneously.

'I can't believe you!' Robert yelled. 'You've ruined my life, taken away my daughter and now you want to drain my bank account!'

'You can't expect me to sign away everything before the divorce when we've had a chance to settle things fairly. What if the judgement goes against me and I have to pay a lot of expenses?'

'Don't be stupid, woman,' huffed Robert. 'How can that happen when we're all as guilty as each other and will all get the same judgement?'

'You can't know that,' I pointed out. 'I've seen some very strange decisions given in the divorce courts. Nothing that happens would surprise me at all.'

Robert paused, calming down.

'All right then,' he agreed suddenly, leaving quickly, I suspected to avoid Terry.

When Terry arrived back late with the prized garage door, I filled him in on what had happened with Robert.

'You did good, girl,' he told me. 'It's about time he realised he can't have everything his own way. You should have asked for more money though. One thousand isn't nearly enough for everything he's put us through.'

'What I don't understand is why Robert is so keen to go,' I said. 'It's only been three months since we came back and we've barely had any time to sell number eight. Now he's demanding we sell number ten without giving us a chance to see how things go.'

I felt especially sorry for Robert having to move because he'd built it himself. My dream home, our beautiful four bedroomed bungalow had been built to our own specifications and was something truly special.

Less than a month later, Robert came round to ask me to sign the papers because he'd found a buyer. Unfortunately, he was one day too late with his request.

~

When we'd started divorce proceeding, Rita and I both agreed that we'd relinquish our share in our respective matrimonial homes, even though my share was worth roughly two thirds more than Rita's. This was because the mortgage on number eight was much higher than the amount it had cost to build number ten, not to mention the fact that number ten was worth more on the open market.

The only reason I had agreed to give up my share was because I'd thought that Rita and Robert would stay put and we'd move away. Robert wanting to sell changed everything, hence my demand for one thousand pounds to agree to the sale, which went against my solicitor's advice.

My solicitor had told me to claim my half share in number ten and let Rita ask for her half of number eight, but, in accordance with my wishes, had written to the other side of my acceptance of the sum of one thousand pounds as my share of number ten should the house be sold.

Robert found a buyer almost within a week of putting number ten on the market.

This is where things became complicated. Unfortunately for Robert, the postman arrived at my door before he did, bringing with him a letter from Rita's solicitor detailing all her earnings over the period of her marriage to Terry. It listed her salaries, dates, etc., and concluded with the line *and so it would appear that our client has a claim in the matrimonial home*.

I was positively fuming and so was Terry. We saw exactly what they were trying to do. They'd hoped to buy me off with one thousand pounds for number ten while plotting to claim Rita's full half share in number eight, which would have amounted to approximately three thousand pounds.

Sheer genius and such a shame their solicitor had written to us before I'd signed away my former home.

Robert knocked on the door with the contract to sell number ten almost immediately after I'd opened his letter. Sometimes I think I could be a successful poker player with my ability to stay calm under pressure and I let none of my anger show on my face as I calmly told him that I couldn't sign anything without the presence of my solicitor and informed him that my solicitor had advised me not to have any further direct communication with him except through my lawyer.

~

I promptly made an appointment to see my solicitor and a few days later, I was sitting in front of him for what turned out to be a very productive meeting.

'Don't worry about your written acceptance of the one thousand pounds, Mrs Andrews,' he reassured me. 'I wrote the clause in such a way that we could rescind it if need be. As it currently stands, your husband is in a very awkward predicament and doesn't have the time to sue over the letter, even if it were possible. He's signed another contract to buy a house a short distance away, so simply cannot afford to argue in court about anything. If he doesn't sort this matter out promptly, he'll be paying for two houses. What would you like me to do?'

It was difficult to contain my glee. 'I think the best thing to do would be to write to Rita's solicitor and tell him that she's more than welcome to her share of number eight and I'll take my fair share of number ten. I think that would be right. Don't you?'

My solicitor agreed to write to the other side with my proposal and all that was left to do was go home and wait for Robert and Rita to open their own bombshell of a letter.

~

I was a nervous wreck waiting for Robert to receive his letter. What would he do when he realised that his plans weren't going as smoothly as he'd have liked? After all, he'd planned to take Terry to the cleaners. Or had he? The thought occurred to us that maybe Rita had gone to the solicitors behind his back to make her claim. We had no idea who was the mastermind behind their failed plan and if Rita *had* gone against Robert's wishes, then I couldn't imagine they'd have a very happy start to their life together.

Nevertheless, we had the upper hand now and they couldn't complete the sale of number ten without my signature, nor could they back out of the new contract they'd signed. We learned that they were planning on moving to a suburb of the Medway Towns and I imagined that with the profits from the sale of the bungalow, they'd easily be able to purchase a nice property, even when you took into account the thousand pounds I was asking for.

The next few days were tense and I scurried out of number eight every morning like a fugitive, escaping to work as quickly as possible. The last thing I wanted was to encounter Robert first thing in the morning. It was only likely to devolve into a shouting match in front of the children.

Three days after my meeting with the solicitor, Robert finally received news of my instructions. My solicitor rang me at work to let me know that my soon to be ex-husband was, to put it mildly, in somewhat of a quandary. Robert had put forward all sorts of solutions to my solicitor to resolve the situation, but my counsel held his ground and things would be done our way or not at all.

The plan was to draw up a legal document for me and Robert to sign in which I agreed to accept one thousand five hundred pounds in settlement for my share of our home. At the same time, he'd also put together a contract for Rita and Terry in which she agreed to accept five hundred pounds as her share of her former home.

My solicitor had thought of everything and insisted that Terry also make a will leaving me a half share in the property, just in case anything happened to him before the divorces were finalised, which could take anything up to two years. After all, once I'd signed away number ten, if something awful happened to Terry before he was officially divorced, Rita could still claim number eight as his legal wife. I'd be left with one thousand pounds and no roof over my head or anywhere to go.

When – and only when – my lawyer's proposals were agreed and carried out, with all documents signed and appropriately exchanged, he'd let me sign the contract to sell number ten.

This seemed perfectly sensible to me and I agreed without hesitation, leaving it to the solicitors to sort out the details.

The delays to Robert's plans caused by my canny solicitor meant that it was another month before Rita and Robert left next door, but they'd gone by late autumn and were settled in their new home in time for Christmas.

Sadly, this also meant John and Sharon starting new schools.

Chapter Twelve

It was Sharon's eighth birthday. After Robert and Rita had moved away, life with Terry had settled into a routine and without the constant reminder next door of my dramatic change in circumstances, life was a little easier and less strained.

I was desperate to keep things civil at least with Robert, wanting the best for the children, so when we were invited to take Sophie and Nicola over for the birthday celebrations, Terry and I jumped at the chance. After all, it gave us the opportunity to see Sharon and John, something that was to prove difficult to arrange. They might only have moved fifteen miles away, but it might as well have been on the other side of the country for how hard it was to arrange visitation. Perhaps Robert and Rita wanted to pretend their first families had never existed; as it was, they never bothered much about trying to see Sophie and Nicola, except for their birthdays.

There was another reason for wanting to go and visit the other couple. Terry and I were both extremely curious about their new home, wondering how much better their new property would be.

'They must have bought quite a splendid place with all the money they got from number ten,' I said to Terry as we were driving over.

'Maybe,' he grunted, keeping his thoughts to himself.

I felt a knot of tension in my stomach, bracing myself to conceal my envy when I saw how much better Robert and Rita were doing than we were.

I could barely conceal my sigh of relief when we pulled up outside a small, three bedroomed, semi-detached house with a wonderful view of the ugly chemical factory opposite. A far cry from my old beautiful, four bedroomed, detached bungalow.

'You all right?' Terry asked me, as he pulled up the handbrake.

I nodded, as we ushered Sophie and Nicola out of the car and in to see their siblings. Robert greeted us curtly, showing us into the small lounge.

Looking around, I noticed that a lot of my old furniture had been replaced with brand new items. They had a dishwasher, a real luxury in those days, a stunning leather three piece suite and various other niceties. It was apparent that rather than investing in a good property, they'd chosen to splash out on new contents.

I found myself having to hide not my jealousy but my surprise. The Robert I knew would have had far more sense than to waste money like that. *Still*, I told myself, *nothing to do with me now.* I'd received my share of the sale and what they did with theirs was up to them.

Nicola gave Sharon her present and the children ran off to play while the grown-ups sat down with a cup of tea. Rita started talking about some of their plans for the property and I only half listened as I absently stirred my tea, doing my best to feign interest.

Suddenly I realised that I was stirring my tea with a little silver apostle spoon. *My* silver apostle spoon. It had been a twenty first birthday present from my beloved aunt Rebecca who had long since passed away. The spoon might not have been worth much as far as money was concerned, but to me it was priceless.

When Robert had put together my belongings after the swap, I hadn't been allowed access to my old home to sort out my things. I'd been forced into trusting that he'd give me everything that was legitimately mine. Foolishly, I believed that Robert had been decent enough to do that, despite what had happened. Now, confronted with my precious spoon, I wondered how many other sentimental mementoes were missing from my life? At the time, I had been too stunned by the speed with which everything had happened to be able to check that I'd got everything I wanted and needed.

I struggled to hold back tears, not wanting to give Robert or Rita the satisfaction of knowing they'd upset me and the rest of the visit passed in a daze. How strange that something as simple as drinking a cup of tea would ram home to me just how much I'd lost. Not only was I dealing with the trauma of losing my son and seeing him brought up by another woman with no control over when I could see him, any trace of my old home had been removed completely as well. Although I had some of my things from number ten – those darned saucepans! – many of my most private, personal things were gone forever.

Still, it had to be said that Rita had upped her game as far as housekeeping was concerned. Their new property was absolutely immaculate and nothing like the disaster she'd left at number eight. Perhaps she was making a special effort on my behalf. After all, who knew when we'd next be invited behind their doors? Still, it was quite a change from the old days, those carefree, innocent days from before the swap, when we'd shared a cleaning lady, my friend Pat. Pat would clean my house every Thursday morning and go round Rita's on a Friday. However, only a few short months later, Pat told me that she couldn't bear to clean Rita's bungalow. 'I simply cannot deal with a house where you have to wipe your feet on your way *out*,' she told me. 'I don't know what that woman does in the week between my visits, but the place is so disgusting I simply can't bring myself to deal with it any longer.'

Either Rita had found a more accommodating cleaner or she'd turned over a new leaf. Certainly, Robert would never tolerate such slovenliness. He'd always been so particular about coming back to a clean, tidy home.

There was a tiny little part of me that hoped that Rita would lapse back to her old ways before long. See how Robert liked dealing with that.

~

I sighed as I saw the post one morning. I could tell without opening the envelopes that Terry had received yet another final demand for an outstanding debt. Recently he'd received a court order for arrears owing on the caravan and I wondered how we were going to meet all our obligations. Although Rita and Robert living on the other side of town made for a less tense home life, we'd decided that we'd go ahead with selling number eight and were doing our best to make it more appealing to buyers. If Robert and Rita could have a fresh start, why couldn't we?

It wasn't easy, though. Even with my money from the settlement, money was tight and when Terry came home that night, I confronted him with the bill.

'Well?' I asked.

'Well, what?'

'What are you going to do about all these bills? I'm ashamed. In all the eleven years I was married to Robert, we never once owed anyone anything, let alone receive a summons. How on earth are we going to cope?'

'Pfft!' Terry waved my concerns away. 'I've been in debt most of my married life. It's no big deal. You pay one bill, another always comes along. It works itself out. You worry far too much.'

'Really?' I arched an eyebrow. 'Well I'll tell you one thing, Terry. I don't care what our situation is. I've never lived in debt and I refuse to start now. You'll just have to sell the caravan and pay off what you owe.'

'Oh come on, Kathy,' protested Terry. 'That caravan's an investment. Think of all the money it saves us on holidays.'

'There won't be any more holidays if you get a court order against you,' I said coldly. 'Get it sold.'

'Can't we at least go away just one more time?' pleaded Terry.

'One more time,' I conceded.

We booked a weekend away and for those couple of days, tried to act as though there was nothing wrong. Terry found it easier to pretend than I – for him, there *wasn't* anything wrong in owing hundreds or thousands of pounds. I couldn't help but worry about what would happen if we couldn't find a buyer for the caravan.

Fortunately, my fears were unwarranted and we were lucky enough to sell it quickly and even have a little bit left over. I'd already worked on improving the property as cheaply as possible. I bought a job lot of cheap wallpaper to freshen up the girls' rooms and gave the place a top to toe makeover with budget paint. As I worked, the place gradually started to look more respectable, tidier and less neglected, the kind of home another couple might want. I finally managed to persuade Terry to clear out the garage and garden shed so that all his unwanted and unusable engine parts, metal, old tools and bric-a-brac were finally gone. With the extra money from the caravan, I was able to tidy up the front garden and with fresh paint on the window and the new-to-us garage door, the place finally looked good enough to call in the agent and get the house on the market.

Ironically, just as we were preparing to move on, I was starting to feel more at home, although there were still times when I'd reach in the cupboard for a particular casserole dish or soup tureen only to remember it was now in Rita's new home.

Terry appreciated the difference a woman's touch could make to a place – if she cared enough to make the effort – and worked hard to support me in keeping things tidy. I started to teach him the simple little tricks of the trade that made it easy to maintain a home and Terry went out of his way to make me happy. There were times when I'd find myself watching him with some little chore around the home and think about how he really was a very considerate and caring person. In the honeymoon period of those first few months, I got to know him better, like him more and surprising myself by even loving him a little.

Certainly, Terry never lost an opportunity to tell me how much he loved me and pressured me to marry as soon as the divorces were final. Every time he asked, I flatly refused. The last thing I needed was more pressure on top of the stress of separation and the reality was that although I might be fond of him, I knew in my heart of hearts that I didn't really love Terry. To be fair, I could have been head over heels in love with him and I still wouldn't have wanted to marry him. I'd had enough of being someone's wife for the time being.

Still, I might not have loved him, but I *did* adore making love with him and we did often, whenever the mood took us and we were alone. The physical side of our relationship only intensified over time, Terry's skills as a lover teaching me new ways of feeling wanted and fulfilled as a woman. Those wonderful moments of ecstasy helped wipe out the traumas of the past few months, if only for a short while, and made life a little more bearable.

However, sex alone is not enough, as I found out to my cost in the years to come.

~

The year flew past and before I knew it, Christmas was approaching. When my parents invited us to spend it with them, I jumped at the opportunity to spend time away with them. They lived about forty miles away on the south coast and, apart from my initial visit to break the news about the swap, I rarely had the chance to see them.

My parents were wonderfully welcoming and it was a refreshing change to be away from number eight, with its tainted memories in every room. My parents' home was large and there was plenty of room for the girls to play while Terry and my family got to know each other a bit better.

Sophie and Nicola played together so naturally, some would have thought that they were sisters. Out of all of us, they seemed to accept the new situation much more easily, probably due to their young ages. Meanwhile, Terry was getting on well with my father, although my sister, Anne, was finding it harder to warm to him. She'd always liked Robert and I could tell that she was more hostile and disapproving of what had happened than the rest of my family. I couldn't blame her. Newly married and blissfully happy, it was hard for her to understand why someone could just walk away from that the way I had.

My younger brother, Edward, was at university and chose to send that Christmas with friends. He knew about what had happened, but we hadn't yet talked about it face to face. I was 13 years older than him and had left home to get married while he was young, so we weren't exactly in close contact.

I had no idea that a strange twist of fate would mean that Edward would play a major role in my life in the not too distant future.

Chapter Thirteen

In January 1973, we had a belated Christmas present when we found a prospective buyer for number eight. Like so many house sales in the UK, finding the buyer was the easy part. The road to exchange and completion was difficult and problematic and full of tension. The last house in a chain of four, we were at the mercy of the other sales. All it would take would be for one purchaser to pull out or have issues and we would all be in trouble.

Of course, we couldn't be so lucky as to have everything go smoothly and the person buying our purchaser's house was struggling to get a mortgage. My heart sank at the prospect of having to start all over again. What made things even more fraught was that we'd heard about a residential caravan for let on a small holiday camp not far away from our house. If we wanted the caravan, we would have to sign the lease before the exchange of contracts and pay rent on it, even though we couldn't move in just yet and may not be able to move in at all if the sale fell through. Should we gamble on the sale completing or lose the caravan? It was a tough decision.

It might sound strange to downgrade from a house to a caravan, but there was a method to our madness. I'd managed to persuade Terry to build a house with me.

Having already built the bungalow at number ten with my soon-to-be-ex-husband and father, I was familiar with the process and wasn't intimidated by the prospect, especially since my Dad was willing to help again with a building project. Building allowed us to enjoy a property much better than anything we could have bought ready built, allowing us to build a house to our exact specifications at a fraction of the price of buying something less than perfect.

The biggest issue when building a property is finding a decent plot of land to build on with planning permission, all within your budget. We'd been looking around for a while and were beginning to despair of finding anything when suddenly we had a shift in fortune.

Perusing the local papers one morning, I spotted an announcement by the county council in the parish where we lived. Thirty plots of land suitable for building were going to be sold by auction in the middle of May. When you buy land at auction, you need to be able to fund the purchase immediately and our second stroke of luck came when we received news of a completion date of 30th March for the sale of number eight.

Everything came together when our new landlord at the caravan site agreed to let us store our furniture in an outbuilding while we lived on the site. For once, things were going our way.

Before we moved, I took the opportunity to sort through everything, keeping only a select few pieces of furniture for our new home. Rita wasn't the only one who could enjoy a brand new suite and I was determined to find the money for as many new items as possible. Somehow.

~

We were left with roughly three thousand pounds after the sale was finalised, nowhere near enough to build our dream home. I made an appointment with Terry's bank manager to see if I could convince him to lend us the money to build our perfect property.

Robert had always dealt with the financial side of things when it came to meetings with managers, so I was somewhat nervous about our discussions. Deciding the best thing to do would be go in as prepared as possible, I sat down and crunched the numbers so I could provide him with detailed calculations for the construction of a bigger-than-average four bedroomed house on one of the plots of land at the forthcoming council auction.

My papers clutched tightly in hand as I waited to meet the manager, I managed to keep a calm exterior that belied my inner nerves. When my name was called, I stepped forward and into the office of Mr Trenton, the Bank Manager.

'And what can I do for you today, Mrs Andrews?' he asked pleasantly.

'Well,' I began. 'As you are no doubt aware, Terry is in the process of divorcing Rita, who is now living with my husband, whom I am divorcing.' Ever the professional, Mr Trenton managed to conceal any surprise or judgement he might be feeling and simply motioned me to carry on. 'We've sold both our houses and while Rita and Robert have bought another property not too far from here, Terry and I would like to build our own. I've done all the calculations so you can see that it makes financial sense.' I passed him the papers I'd brought with me and I held my breath while he looked over them.

'Could you tell me some more about the financial arrangement you have with Mr Andrews and Mrs Farmer?' Mr Trenton asked.

'Of course. We came to an agreement through our solicitors to grant Rita and myself a fair share of our respective properties and my solicitor has arranged an iron clad contract so that should anything untoward happen to Terry, I'll still be entitled to keep my home.'

'And the divorce isn't yet settled?'

'Not yet,' I shook my head.

'Impressive. I must commend you on your choice of solicitor,' he smiled.

We talked through what I wanted: a temporary loan, enough to enable us to bid for a plot and buy some building materials.

'I'm not saying yes to the loan, but on the other hand, I'm not saying no either,' Mr Trenton finally concluded. 'I'll need to take this one to my superiors, but I'll argue your case as well as I can and hopefully we'll have an answer for you one way or another within the next couple of weeks.'

'Thank you so much for your time,' I said, standing to shake his hand in farewell. Cautiously optimistic about our chances, when I received a letter asking me to attend another meeting at the bank two weeks later, I convinced Terry to accompany me this time to hear the news.

'Ah, Mr Farmer, Mrs Andrews,' beamed Mr Trenton. 'Wonderful news. We've got your loan! Quite frankly, I didn't hold out much hope, but the powers that be have agreed and all that remains now is to finalise a few pieces of paperwork and the money's all yours.'

From the level of his enthusiasm, you'd think it was he who had just had a loan approved, and now we had the support of Terry's bank to buy our plot of land, I had renewed hope that everything would run smoothly from now on.

~

One of the reasons why I was so optimistic was because I'd also noticed another advertisement for land offered for sale by tender in a nearby town. I thought it made good sense to try our luck with both opportunities, because the timings of the sales meant that if I were successful with one, I wouldn't need to worry about the other.

Luckily, I had an old friend who was a local council officer, and I asked him for his advice on the best way for us to become landowners once more. He gave me two invaluable pieces of advice, the first being to add a few more pounds to our offer, since the vendors are bound by law to take the highest bid. Since people normally think in terms of round figures when it comes to putting forward an offer, those few extra pounds could make all the difference between success and failure.

Secondly, he recommended that we bid on all the available lots, ten in total of varying sizes. His reasoning was that since all the lots had a reserve price on them, our bid might be too low for one, but we could still be successful with another.

Since all the plots came with planning permission in a fantastic location, I was determined to do my best to win one of them, and I told Mr Trenton that I would be putting in a bid of five thousand and thirteen pounds for the land, five thousand being our maximum limit. In a strange twist of superstition, I thought that thirteen might prove to be lucky for us.

Unfortunately, I was wrong, and we were unsuccessful with our tender, all the plots fetching far more than we could ever afford. With a heavy heart, I went down to the bank to let Mr Trenton know what had happened.

Mr Trenton was unavailable when I arrived, so I spoke to the Under-Manager, Mr Connor. 'I've got bad news,' I informed him. 'Mr Farmer and I put in a bid for a number of plots but didn't manage to secure any of them, so we need to extend our loan to cover the auction in a couple of weeks.'

Mr Connor frowned. 'I'm sorry to hear that. However, it is our policy not to automatically extend loans. You'll need to reapply and I can't guarantee that you'll be successful a second time. Still, you never know. Let me fetch you the forms.'

My heart sank. If we didn't get approval in time for the auction, we'd be struggling and who knew how long we'd have to live in the caravan then?

'Mrs Andrews!' A jovial voice came from behind. I turned to see Mr Trenton passing. 'How did it go with the tender?'

'I was just explaining to Mr Connor that we didn't get any of the lots,' I said sadly. 'He was just getting me the forms to reapply for a loan.'

'Oh, no need for that.' Mr Trenton waved away my concerns. 'The loan is yours for six months. Go out and find another piece of land.' He shook my hand and I virtually skipped out of the bank, counting my good fortune that he'd happened by at that moment. Had I listened to the Under-Manager, I might have given up all hope of buying somewhere. Our project was back on course and the next step was to go to the auction in two weeks' time.

~

If I'd expected Terry to be as excited as I was, I was in for a disappointment. 'I don't know why you're bothering,' he grumbled when I gave him the good news. 'You're just building castles in the air. It was a stupid idea in the first place. People like us don't build houses.'

'Don't be like that,' I told him. 'Whatever happened to having a positive attitude? I've done it before and I can do it again. We've got six months to find something and I'll make sure we do. We've got that auction coming up. You never know what might happen there.'

'Yes I do,' he replied. 'Nothing, because I'm not going.'

'Oh come on, Terry,' I sighed. 'I need you there to help make sure we get the right plot.'

'I'm not going,' he repeated. 'If you want to do this, you're on your own.'

'Fine. I'll go on my own then,' I retorted and set about researching property auctions so I'd stand the best possible chance of winning a lot.

I ordered the prospectus of plots for sale. There were about twenty, of which three were suitable for our budget. Building land was very scarce in the south east of England, even back then, so an auction of this type attracted dealers and builders from all over the place. When I walked in to find a seat, I discovered a packed hall, bustling with excitement. I found myself caught up in a wave of nervous anticipation. Bidding hadn't even started and already I could understand why people went over their budget. I swore to myself that I would stick to my limit.

'Ladies and gentlemen, could you please all come to order. The auction is about to start!' announced the auctioneer. He explained the rules and the requirement that any successful bidder would need to pay ten per cent of the price now, with the balance due within a month of the auction.

Terry and I had picked out plot number three for our first attempt and I figured it would make a good practice run for the other two lots. Watching plots one and two go under the gavel, the first thing that struck me was the speed of the proceedings. How on earth would I manage to keep track of it all and not accidentally bid more than I should?

All too soon, plot number three was announced and I braced myself for action.

'Who will start with £3,500?' came the call.

I put my hand up.

'With you at the back sir. 4,000.'

I craned my neck to see who'd counter offered and missed the next bid.

'With you sir on my left.'

This is a fix, I thought. *I don't stand a chance.*

'Now who will give me 4,250?'

I decided to be brave and try one more time, putting up my hand.

'With you in the front, madam.'

I braced myself for a higher bid, knowing that there wasn't much left in my budget. To my surprise, the bidding stopped, the hammer went down and I found myself the owner of a piece of land.

The remaining plots were sold with lots of frantic calling and bidding, but I paid no attention to it. *I was the owner of a piece of land!*

Once the excitement wore off, reality sank in. What had I done? We hadn't even inspected the plots before the auction and I had no idea about the location, the view or anything else we should have considered.

Still, what was done, was done and after the auction ended, I joined the queue of successful bidders waiting to pay their deposit to the officer in charge. While standing there, I spotted a builder that I knew in passing, someone Robert had worked with on occasion.

'Why hello, Mrs Andrews,' he smiled. 'You building another property?'

'That's the plan,' I replied.

'Well, good luck to you. Robert always did have a good eye for what works.'

I said nothing, merely smiling politely.

'So what plot did you get?' he asked.

'Number three,' I replied. 'Why?'

He sucked air through his teeth, shaking his head. 'I hope you know what you're taking on,' he warned me. 'Did you realise that the drains are twenty feet down the road there?'

I shook my head.

'You'll need your own pumping station to make any new property viable and do you know how costly that is?'

Once more, I shook my head.

He thought for a moment and then said 'tell you what. If you like, I'll purchase the land instead of you and save you making a big mistake.'

If it's such a bad plot, why does he want it? I thought, saying out loud 'no thanks. I'll wait until I've spoken to my husband.'

'You just let me know if you change your mind,' he told me. 'Here's my number. I'll take it off your hands.'

It was my turn to pay my deposit, putting an end to our conversation and as soon as I was done, I rushed back to see Terry at work, too excited to wait until he got home.

'Well?' he asked as soon as he saw me.

'We got it!' I squealed. Terry picked me up and spin me round, both of us over the moon and scarcely able to believe our luck.

I told Terry all about the builder wanting to buy our plot and we decided that the first thing we needed to do was to find out what exactly we'd bought, then go to the council planning department offices to see just how bad the drainage situation was. Terry clocked off for the afternoon and we both drove over to see the site of our potential new home.

We pulled up outside a nice level plot about 100 feet long and 40 feet wide, more than enough to build a modest detached house on. Spotting a small café nearby, we popped in for a celebratory lunch while we waited for the council offices to open. The stewed tea could have been champagne as far as we were concerned, too happy to care about what we were eating and drinking. Reality was starting to sink in and the fact was that we'd bought our piece of land, which, as far as I was concerned, was the first and biggest hurdle we had to jump in order to have our dream home.

At last the council offices were open and a very helpful young lady showed us the site plans of all the plots. We could immediately see that fortune had smiled on us yet again and the main drainage line was, in fact, running alongside the length of our plot. Far from being a problem, we had only to run from the side of the house straight into the drain, a matter of twenty feet at the most. So much for costly pumping stations!

Within a month, our purchase was complete and since I hadn't used my entire budget buying the land, I had enough money left over to order bricks and block for the building. This was doubly crucial because this was the year of the three day week, thanks to strike action by the miners, a big dispute that sent shock waves throughout industry, so building materials were just one of many commodities in short supply.

~

Thus began a very busy, but highly productive, time for us. We moved into the rented caravan, lock, stock and Labrador, and life in our new surroundings was surprisingly comfortable, even though it was a bit of a tight squeeze.

We found an architect we liked who drew up plans for our ideal home, including four bedrooms and a bathroom upstairs as well as a kitchen-diner, lounge, utility room and shower room downstairs. Terry also got his wish for a large double garage for his many side lines working from home repairing cars and the like.

With every day, our vision moved that little bit closer to reality and we even managed to entertain friends in the caravan on occasion, turning our temporary accommodation into a home of sorts.

Before construction began, I acquired a cheap old caravan to be used as our site office as well as a job lot of used scaffolding – minus boards – for the very reasonable sum of sixty pounds. I wasn't to know it at the time, but the latter proved to be a sound investment, as a few friends were inspired by our home building journey to follow in our footsteps. This enabled us to get our carpentry and plumbing work done with free labour in exchange for the use of our scaffolding on their own projects. When our house was complete, I then managed to sell on the equipment to another friend for the princely sum of two hundred and fifty pounds, money that helped when it came to furnishing the place.

Surprising myself with just how adept I was at financial matters, I also set in motion our application for a stage payment mortgage with the council who'd sold us the land. Perhaps my time with Robert had taught me a few tricks of the trade after all. Our new mortgage would allow us to build the house to a certain stage, apply for a percentage of the mortgage to build the next step and so on and so on until the house was finished and the final instalment paid.

We applied for a four thousand pound mortgage at eleven per cent, fixed for a twenty five year repayment term, and got it with very little difficulty. We were moving up in the world!

Chapter Fourteen

It's amazing what being busy can do to keep your mind off things and Terry and I were so caught up in the intricacies of buying land and moving that we barely thought about the other couple in our lives or even the children.

At the beginning of June 9173, a letter landed on our mat. Terry read it with a wry smile on his face. 'The hearing for our divorces is happening on June 26th in Canterbury,' he told me. 'Our anniversary.'

How ironic I thought.

We were required to arrive at ten o'clock in the morning and the week before the hearing, we visited our solicitor to go over the details of the case and discuss any potential difficulties he'd highlighted.

'I'm warning you now,' he told us, 'getting your divorces isn't going to be easy.'

'Why not?' asked Terry. 'I would have thought it would be pretty obvious we don't want to be married to our spouses, since we're both living with someone else.'

'Ah,' exclaimed our lawyer. 'And therein lies the problem. Since you're applying for divorce on the grounds of adultery, the fact that you've all agreed to the swap may well render such a claim null and void. The judge will ask *how can a man agree to his wife sleeping with another man, thus allowing her to commit adultery, and then turn around and say that he wants a divorce because his wife has been adulterous?'*

My heart sank. I'd been told this before, but I had hoped that our solicitor would have found some way around it.

'It is entirely possible that you could end up with no divorce this time around and have to wait for another two years and petition for divorce on the grounds of separation,' he warned us.

I sighed, but at least we were prepared for the worst and if we had to wait two years, then so be it.

'There's an additional complication with the arrangement you've made for the children,' he continued. 'The courts don't like it when siblings are separated, so keeping one child each may not be permitted in the final settlement. It is entirely possible they might decide that all four children need to stay together in one family.'

'They couldn't!' I gasped.

'I'm afraid they could,' said my solicitor grimly.

'What are the chances of that happening?' asked Terry.

'It's hard to say.' He shrugged his shoulders. 'We'll just have to wait and see.'

On the way home, neither Terry nor I had much to say, both of us deep in thought. The notion of all four children in one household filled me with dread. I couldn't imagine Rita coping with all of them and I wouldn't want to be separated from Sophie. However, the thought of all four with us was an equally frightening prospect.

I knew that Terry would be over the moon to have the children with us, but it wasn't him who would have to deal with all the washing, cooking and cleaning. I wouldn't be able to cope, but I didn't think Terry would take kindly to my pointing this out. Could this mean battles at home as well as in the court room?

This wasn't the first time during divorce proceedings that the children had caused us problems. Initially, Robert had said that he'd apply for custody of our two children, giving care and control of Sophie to me. I didn't have a problem with this because our solicitor explained that if Robert had custody of both, this made him legally responsible for their wellbeing, so I could apply for help with maintenance in the future without needing to go back to court, an arrangement that sat well with me.

Rita wasn't nearly as agreeable when it came to Nicola and Sharon. When the same idea was proposed to her, awarding care and control of Nicola to Terry, she turned it down. The parent awarded custody would need to provide financially for the child in question, while care and control meant actually looking after the child on a daily basis.

Angry, and wanting to pressure Rita, Terry told me to threaten Robert with demanding both custody and care of control of Sophie and John if Rita wouldn't see sense. I point blank refused, telling him that my children were not to be used as pawns in our game just so that he could have access to Nicola. I didn't want to battle with Robert over my children just to bring Rita in line.

Fortunately, Rita eventually saw sense and our divorces were scheduled to be heard one after the other, with us all making equal claims in all respects.

I decided that I needed a boost in confidence and treated myself to a brand new outfit for one of the most important days of my life. After all, nothing makes you feel better than new clothes and wearing my smart new skirt and blouse, I felt ready to face anything.

I arranged for friends to pick up the children from school at four o'clock so that there was no extra pressure. Although our cases were due in the morning, I'd been warned that courts could be in a world of their own when it came to timing and it was a relief to know that there were no time pressures.

Terry and I arrived at the court house nice and early and parked in the long stay car park before meandering over to the court building. We were shown into an antechamber to meet with our solicitor and barrister and as we waited for the men to arrive, I felt myself start to sweat, becoming very nervous at the thought of meeting the other two halves. We hadn't dealt with them much in the few months since they'd moved away, and I wondered whether they'd bear us any grudges after the drama of selling number ten.

As it turned out, I had nothing to fear. Robert and Rita came through the door, Rita looking as glamourous as ever, and headed straight towards us, greeting us like old friends they'd been looking forward to seeing for ages, rather than the soon-to-be-ex-spouses we really were. As we made small talk, no one watching could ever have guessed that we were all there to divorce each other.

At last, the court doors were opened and we took seats together, listening with interest to the three minor civil cases that came before us. It was a glorious summer's day and I felt very sorry for the judge in his heavy black gown. He was very old and frail looking and his clothes and wig seemed to weigh heavy upon his ancient shoulders. He appeared to be very under the weather and I hoped that wouldn't affect his mood when it came to hearing our petition.

At last, Terry was called to the stand and I watched as he was sworn in on the Bible, just like a scene out of a Perry Mason movie. His barrister launched into the standard questions, asking Terry why he wanted to divorce Rita. As instructed, he replied that it was because of her adulterous association with Mr Robert Andrews and it was only a matter of minutes before the judge awarded Terry his decree nisi. Since we'd already dealt with the property issues, there were only the children to decide upon and Terry and Rita were awarded joint custody of Sharon and Nicola.

Terry came down from the stand, returning to his seat in the pew next to me and he gave my arm a quick squeeze of reassurance, unable to hide the happy smile on his face.

Robert was up next and his ashen faced demeanour was in stark contrast to Terry's confidence. His barrister was a young man who gave me the distinct impression that he hadn't been qualified for long and when he started questioning Robert, he was soon interrupted by the judge.

'I'm sorry,' the old man said. 'But it seems to me that this case has a close connection with the case I've just given judgement on. Is that correct?'

'It is,' confirmed Robert's brief.

'Hmmm,' frowned the judge. 'That being the situation, I'm going to adjourn this case until after lunch and I want all associated parties to present themselves before me at two o'clock. Furthermore, I rescind the decision I gave in the last case until this mess is sorted out.'

The court rose as the judge left, the room abuzz with excitement at this dramatic turn of events.

'I think we've just made legal history,' exclaimed my solicitor. 'I've never heard of this happening before. To award a divorce and then take it back immediately is incredible. Suppose you'd left the court after your case? You'd be on your way back home right now under the impression you're divorced when you're not.' He shook his head in amazement. 'Go and have lunch,' he advised, 'and make sure you're back here for two o'clock on the dot. I suggest you *don't* come back breathing alcohol fumes everywhere. Meanwhile, I'll find their barrister and put him straight on a few matters.'

He rushed off in search of the other barrister, while we went out to find somewhere to eat, passing Rita on the way. She was very agitated, and not just because of what had happened. Robert had left his car on a parking meter, thinking everything would be straightforward, and needed to move it before he got a ticket.

We discovered a little restaurant close to the court where the legal teams clearly liked to dine, and ordered a snack lunch. Although we'd been advised against alcohol, Terry had a beer while I treated myself to a small glass of wine. We both needed it. Just as we'd been warned, this was turning into a complicated divorce and it was beginning to look as though we'd be back in two years after all.

Halfway through our meal, our solicitor arrived.

'Right,' he said. 'I've spoken to the other side's solicitor to update him on a few points of law concerning your situation. Believe it or not, Robert and Rita haven't been entirely honest with him about what happened, which has complicated things unnecessarily. Had they been upfront like you two, we might have avoided this situation.

'According to their version of events, you four all went on holiday together where the swap took place with no previous agreements. Understandably, their solicitor thought the divorce was a simple open and shut case based on your behaviour, Mrs Andrews.'

I blushed and shook my head in disbelief.

'I've put them in the picture with all the facts as you've provided them and given the other side some advice about the best line of questioning when we return to court,' my solicitor went on, 'but their barrister is young and inexperienced, so it's hard to tell whether he'll follow my lead.'

'So what's going to happen?' asked Terry anxiously. 'Do you think we'll get our divorces today?'

'I genuinely couldn't say.' Our solicitor shrugged his shoulders. 'Anything might happen now. I mean, I've never before heard of a judge rescinding a divorce he'd granted thirty minutes earlier.' He glanced up at the clock. 'We'd better get back to court now. It's quarter to two and we don't want to annoy the judge by being late.'

We entered the chamber to see Robert's solicitor and barrister huddled over large tomes, frantically making notes to help their case.

'I don't think they've had any lunch,' I whispered to Terry.

'Serves them right,' he replied. 'They should have got their act together sooner.'

As the court room began to fill, Robert and Rita took their seats, looking very subdued and anxious.

'The court will rise,' bellowed an usher and the judge came in to take his seat at the head of the room. Robert returned to the stand and we began again.

Before Robert was asked to speak, the judge and young barrister battled it out to see whether the divorce could proceed. It seemed to me that His Lordship was taking great delight in giving this egotistical young legal expert a lesson in doing your homework. He'd put over a point of law by quoting a precedent from memory, forcing the barrister to refer to his law books before answering.

As the judge threw out his jabs, the poor barrister gradually worked his way through the books, running out of pages to turn to. However, after twenty minutes of this verbal sparring, the judge finally put the man out of his misery and allowed him to return to his cross-examination of Robert.

'Why do you want to divorce your wife, Kathy?' asked the barrister.

'Because she doesn't love me any more,' replied Robert. I groaned. This answer wasn't correct and not what the judge was waiting to hear.

'I repeat, Mr Andrews, why do you want to divorce your wife?'

'Because she doesn't want to live with me any more.'

Yet again, the wrong reply.

The barrister tried a third time and finally heard the words he needed to hear. 'I want to divorce Kathy because of her adulterous association with Mr Terry Farmer.'

Having uttered those important words, the judge raised his hands and brought an end to the proceedings. To my amazement, he granted decree nisi to Robert, reinstating Terry's. He beckoned Robert's barrister to approach and after a brief discussion, announced that he was awarding joint custody of our children to Robert and I, giving care and control of Sophie to me and John to Robert.

At last it was over and the respective counsels gathered up their papers and books before we all filed out of the courtroom and back to the ante chamber. Terry and I were given our decree nisi for our records and told that although we were now legally divorced, we'd need to wait approximately six more weeks for our decree absolutes before we were free to remarry.

We shook hands with our solicitor, thanking him profusely, before starting the journey home. We were both silent in the car, the events of the day impacting on us both. I thought to myself how glad I was that I'd made arrangements for the children or I'd be worrying about their whereabouts along with everything else.

And so it was that what had been conceived as a bit of fun, a way to inject a bit of excitement into our suburban lives, had resulted in the break-up of two families. When

I started out on this escapade, I never thought it would come to this. Never in a million years had I thought that I'd live with Terry and the speed with which it had all happened was stunning. It was less than a year since we'd been on that fateful holiday and now we were all divorced.

We picked up the children from my friend and went home for tea. Although the girls were young, we decided that it was best to explain to them what had happened so they wouldn't be hurt any more than necessary.

As the children tucked into their supper, I gently explained that we were now a new family, although they would still see their siblings and other parents. I was careful to reassure them that we would always do our best to make sure they kept in contact with the other half as much as possible and although they were too young to fully comprehend the permanency of what had happened, I felt that I did the right thing in being open and honest with the girls.

In later years, throughout the heartbreak and misery that occurred, the one thing that kept me going was my darling Sophie. She assured me on more than one occasion that she'd felt a lot more stable knowing that I'd kept her in my confidence about everything that was going on and was very grateful I'd taken the trouble to include her in our decisions. A small comfort, perhaps, but one that meant a great deal.

Chapter Fifteen

Now that the unpleasantness of divorce was out of the way, Terry and I were free to throw all our efforts into building our new home. I negotiated a fair price with my father and brothers for them to do the brickwork on our house and my father also agreed to help us with the preliminary work involved in laying out the foundations.

Our plans were approved at the end of July and now that we had the go-ahead, building began in earnest. I arranged for an excavator and driver to start digging out the foundations on August Bank Holiday 1973. Having grown up in a family of builders and already been through one construction project with Robert, I knew quite a lot about building, but I still found myself turning to my father for advice and assistance, which he was more than happy to offer, especially since Terry's background was in engineering, so needed expert input.

One day, the 'other family' came to pick up the girls for a day out, taking the opportunity to have a nose about our site. The foundations had been dug and the over site was ready for concreting, so I had no qualms about showing Robert the plans. If he'd hoped to find us struggling, he was sorely disappointed, and I think he was more than a little surprised to find that we'd managed to start building.

Our new property was going to be more spacious and ambitious than the little bungalow Robert and I had built two years before and I wondered what was going through his mind as he looked over our plans. I still couldn't believe that he actually wanted us to be divorced so that he could live with Rita, but I said nothing, putting the plans away in the caravan and returning to work, while Robert and Rita took the girls on their trip.

~

Once the foundations were all ready and the council had approved them, the shell of the building was put up in a mere six weeks. My father did me proud, and I did my best to support him in his work by making sure that they were never short of building materials. 1973 was the winter of discontent and the coal miner's strike and three day week had caused all sorts of problems, especially in the building industry.

One particular incident worked in my favour. A very good builder friend had advised me that since plaster was in short supply, I should order twice what I actually needed, since I'd probably only get half my order. As a result, needing one ton, I ordered two tons of plaster, to be delivered in paper sacks like cement. Imagine my surprise when, after a short delay, two tons of plaster arrived. Seeing an opportunity, I was able to sell our surplus to local builders for a nice little profit. Every penny helped.

Once the brickwork was complete up to roof level, we were able to apply for our first mortgage stage payment, enabling me to buy all the roof trusses and tile the roof. Building was progressing smoothly and by Christmas, we'd completed the shell of the building, with the roof on, windows in and first fixings of plumbing and electrics.

~

Meanwhile, in October 1973, Robert and Rita got married. Their witness was a friend of Robert's who'd been the best man at our wedding and it was a relatively lavish affair, with John wearing his first grown up suit and Sharon as Rita's bridesmaid. Her only bridesmaid.

As I comforted Nicola, I reflected on how insensitive it had been of Rita to ask one daughter and not the other. Were our situations reversed, I would have invited both or neither and Terry was absolutely livid at this treatment of his beloved daughter, but what could we do? It wasn't our wedding.

As it was, we had other things to worry about. With Christmas fast approaching, the cramped conditions in the caravan were posing a problem. We wanted to make sure that Sophie and Nicola enjoyed themselves for this first Christmas following the divorces. I'd bought the girls a doll's pram each as their main present and the caravan barely afforded enough room to open their presents, let alone play with them.

I asked Robert and Rita if the girls could spend Christmas day with them. It seemed the simplest solution to the problem, yet the reply came back as a firm no, with no specific reason given. I couldn't even speculate what was going through the newlyweds' minds. Fortunately, a workmate of Terry's invited us to his home for Christmas day, so the girls had a brilliant time in the end, but this wasn't the first time a difference in attitude towards childcare caused a rift between the families and it wouldn't be the last.

~

Work progressed nicely on the new house and by January 1974, we were ready to plaster. This is one of the stages of house building I like the least. There are a hundred and one things to do before you can plaster and the process seems to take forever. However, once it was finished, the house began to look liveable in and I could start to see it as a home.

Finally, we were ready for the expensive stage of finishing. My eye for a good deal served us in good stead once again, as we found second hand bargains, such as the fittings for the utility room. A plumber friend gave us some unwanted tiles while I bagged fifteen gallons of white emulsion from the factory for just fifty pence a gallon.

Incredibly, the house was ready for us to move in by the end of March, a mere six months after starting work. It wasn't completely finished: doors still had to be hung and painted; flooring needed to be laid; tiling had to be done; not to mention all the painting and decorating. Still, we finally had a place to call home and could leave behind the cramped caravan.

It felt as though we were living in a palace after such small quarters, our few bits and pieces of furniture seeming lost and adrift in the large rooms. Still, it didn't take long to buy a new three piece suite, dining table and chairs and a bedroom suite for Terry and me. The girls' rooms were furnished with various bits and pieces we found in the local paper and we settled down to begin our new life.

Things were looking up financially too. We received the final payment of the mortgage, even though the property wasn't entirely complete, having satisfied the council's building surveyor that the four thousand pound mortgage was more than covered by the value of the property as it was. We used some of that money to pay the deposit on a new car and everything seemed to be going well. At last, I could let myself feel happiness after the trauma of the last two years. Our debts had all been paid, giving me more security, and I could look at everything we'd achieved together and feel pride in our accomplishments. Even better, Terry started a new job as a fitter at a local steel mill, bringing more money into the household.

I felt so confident that things were going right for a change that when Terry suddenly proposed, in a moment of madness, I agreed.

Part of the reason for my change of heart was the advice from our accountant, who said that we should marry for tax purposes. A ring on my finger would also allow me to claim family allowance, so my motives weren't entirely romantic. Still, my agreeing was a major change of heart for me, having previously made it plain that under no circumstances would I consider remarrying, but now that we had our home, it seemed to make sense to tied up the loose ends and become a proper family.

Our wedding was a simple affair. I bought a new outfit at the last minute from the market for a mere five pounds and my sister Anne and her husband were our witnesses. We were wed at the Registry Office in the high street next to Tesco, so after the ceremony, it seemed to make perfect sense to nip next door to do the weekly shopping. I ignored the funny looks I got, covered in confetti as I was with flowers in my hair. In that moment, I was happy.

The four of us went out for a celebratory evening meal and then the next morning it was back to work as usual, almost as if nothing had happened. I didn't feel that we needed a honeymoon and didn't really want one, not second time around.

~

The following three years were the happiest Terry and I spent together. We gradually finished all the little jobs around the house, which we named 'Windermere' for sentimental reasons, since that's where we'd spent our night away during that ill-fated holiday. The girls were well adjusted and enjoyed each other's company; they were both achieving good grades in school, too.

We invited John and Sharon to stay with us for our first Christmas at Windermere and it was easy to forget the tears that had brought us to this moment, as the six of us enjoyed a cheerful holiday together. Terry and I always liked to see our other two children as often as possible and did our best to keep on good terms with Rita and Robert. I always believed that we should try to at least maintain an appearance of a cordial relationship with them for the sake of the children. Nobody should witness their parents fighting and pulling each other to pieces.

As a consequence, I did my best not to criticise Rita or attempt to influence John in any way, other than to encourage him to accept Rita as his new mother and do his best to behave, despite everything that had happened

It broke my heart to push him away like that, especially when I opened the door to him one afternoon. He'd cycled all that way with a friend to surprise me.

'Does your father know you've come here?' I asked.

'No. I just came over on the spur of the moment,' he replied.

Although I was secretly proud of my son, touched that he would cycle ten miles just to see his old Mum, I was also worried about him travelling all that way without an adult. He was only thirteen, after all.

I invited him in for tea and phoned Robert to let him know that our son was safe. I subsequently found out that he was punished for the visit. He was grounded for a whole month, a little harsh, I felt, for a lad who'd just wanted to see his Mum. Still, I bit my tongue, leaving it to the other two to parent my son as they saw fit.

However, I couldn't stay quiet over arrangements concerning Sharon. During our second summer at Windermere, Terry's sister, Marion, was due to visit and I rang to see if Sharon could come to see her on the Saturday.

Robert answered the phone. 'I'm not sure,' was his initial reaction. 'We're going to visit my mother that day.'

'Well, couldn't you leave Sharon with us and visit your mother with just John for once? It might be nice for her to spend some time alone with her grandson,' I suggested.

Robert thought for a moment. 'I don't see why not,' he finally agreed. 'Sharon's not my mother's favourite. Yes, that seems reasonable. I'll have to okay it with Rita first though. I'll get back to you.'

I hung up on a perfectly amicable conversation, confident that Terry would be able to enjoy having both of his daughters with him for Marion's visit. My good mood was completely shattered when Rita rang back later.

'I'm sorry, but you'll have to manage without Sharon,' she informed me loftily. 'We're a family now. John and Sharon are brother and sister and they go everywhere together.'

'That's ridiculous!' I protested. 'Does that mean that when he's sixteen and she's thirteen, he's got to take her with him everywhere?'

'Now listen here, you narrow minded bitch,' she began, but I had no interest in listening to abuse. I hung up on her, unwilling to be insulted and not clever enough to answer her back.

I went into the kitchen and began peeling potatoes for dinner, angry tears pricking at the corners of my eyes. How could she be so cruel? Her reaction to a perfectly reasonable request was to attack me because underneath it all, she objected to the fact that Robert and I had agreed on something without consulting her.

Not long after, the phone rang again. It was Rita, of course, asking to speak to Marion. I handed the phone over without a word and it was clear from Marion's expression that Rita had picked up from where she left off with me. However, in the end, she agreed to let Sharon come over alone for the day; happy, no doubt, that she'd caused enough upset to make her point.

How nasty and spiteful when Rita knew all along that she and Robert would be packing up and moving to Derbyshire within the month.

Chapter Sixteen

Despite all the planning and preparation it must have taken, Robert and Rita managed to keep everything a secret until a mere two weeks before they moved up north. Just before the start of the new school year, Terry answered the phone. It was Rita.

'I just thought I'd give you a call to let you know that Robert's been on a few job interviews,' she informed Terry.

'OK,' he replied, wondering where this was leading.

'He's been offered positions in London and Derby,' she continued.

'Lucky Robert!' commented Terry.

'Well, I decided that it would be best for Robert to accept the post in Derby. We'll be moving in two weeks' time. Robert and I are heading up to Derbyshire this coming Saturday to sort the house out ready for our move.'

I could tell from Terry's face that something major had happened and couldn't wait for him to finish the call so I could find out what.

'Can we have the children this weekend?' I heard him ask and he hung up after Rita agreed.

'What's happened?' I asked anxiously.

'Rita and Robert are moving to the other end of the country,' he gasped, still visibly stunned.

My heart sank. Now we would be lucky to see John and Sharon in the school holidays. We barely saw enough of them as it was. Once they'd moved two hundred miles away, how would we ever co-ordinate visits?

'Why on earth would they want to move like that?' I wondered. 'Do they really think that being ten miles away is too close for comfort?'

'I don't know,' shrugged Terry. 'Maybe things aren't going too well between them and they want to get as far away from us as possible.'

'What about Sharon?' I asked. 'I know Rita's been having a few problems with her. Does she really think that taking her so far away from her Dad will solve all that?'

Terry sighed and shook his head.

~

We made the most of our last weekend, taking the opportunity to spoil the children a little. Who knew when the four of them would all be together again?

When it was time to say goodbye, I fought back tears, refusing to break down in front of the kids. It was hard enough for us all to see them go; I didn't want to add to it. 'You be good,' was all I could say.

We missed the children terribly, but somehow managed to carry on with our lives, booking an expensive holiday camp on the south coast for us all the following summer. Sophie and Nicola also spent a week up in Derbyshire over the school break, but Sophie was reluctant to go on the visits because she couldn't cope with seeing her father being so distant. When they first moved, she used to look forward to seeing Robert, wanting to be with him just like any normal eight year old, only to be disappointed by his cold, off-hand manner. She couldn't understand why her father couldn't be natural with her like Terri was with Nicola and it didn't help that she clashed with Rita.

At first, Sophie wrote to her father, long letters full of little stories about her life. On one occasion, I remember her pleading with him to write back. *Please, please, please write to me,* she ended one letter in a desperate attempt to provoke some kind of reaction from him.

The next thing I knew, Rita was on the phone, chastising me. 'You know, she's a naughty girl to keep worrying her father like this,' she said. 'As if Robert doesn't have enough on his plate.'

I was speechless and angry with myself for not immediately defending Sophie. I could always think of the things I should have said after I hung up, but faced with Rita's smug, superior nature, I never knew the best thing to do to take her down a peg or two.

Still, if I was having problems with Sophie, it was nothing compared to the difficulties they were having with Sharon, trouble we knew nothing about.

~

In the spring of 1977, while Rita and I were discussing arrangements for John and Sharon to come and stay for the Easter holidays, Rita confessed that she was very worried about Sharon. 'I hate to admit it,' she told me, 'but there's been more than one time when I felt like bringing her down and just leaving her on your doorstep. I'm rapidly coming to the end of my tether when it comes to that girl.'

Fool that I was, like an insect flying into the spider's web, I said 'well if she's that unhappy, maybe she should come and live with us. After all, the children are the innocent victims in this break up and I don't see why they should suffer.'

With my ill thought offer, I sealed the fate of my second marriage.

'Could she?' asked Rita in delight. 'That would be wonderful. Sharon will be so happy. I'll talk to Robert and we'll make the final arrangements. Thank you so much!'

Sharon came to live with us permanently in the summer of 1977. I already knew it wouldn't be easy adjusting to a third girl in the house. I'd never enjoyed the same level of closeness with Sharon that I had with Nicola.

Our next summer holiday that year was memorable for the sheer misery of it. We hired a caravan and booked ourselves into a campsite in the Lake District for two weeks, picking up the girls from Derby, where they had spent two weeks previously.

We arrived in time for tea and sent the girls off to explore the site whilst we erected the awning. I'd noticed Nicola scratching her hair on the journey up and when she came back for supper, I called her over. 'Let me take a look at you,' I said, examining her thick mop of curly hair. Imagine my horror when I saw that her head was crawling with lice.

I called Terry over to take a look. 'What on earth can we do?' I asked, but Terry had no suggestions. It was August Bank Holiday Saturday and all the shops would be shut until Tuesday.

I checked the other girls' heads but they were clear. However, with us all sleeping together in a caravan in close proximity, it was a foregone conclusion that we'd all suffer the same fate.

Out of desperation, I hit upon the idea of spraying their heads with fly killer and getting them to put on their anoraks with the hood up, zipped up tight to the neck, in the hope that it might do something to stop the little critters. Poor Nicola was most distressed and in one photo taken on a boat trip on the Sunday, you've never seen a more miserable looking child. She looked just how I felt.

It seemed that caravan holidays were always going to spell disaster for me and I made sure to be outside the chemist's early on Tuesday morning before they'd even opened. Terry had refused to accompany me, leaving me to explain our predicament to the shop assistant. Too ashamed to admit the truth, I told her that the problem had been with the caravan we hired, when in fact it had been spotless when we'd collected it from a friend. Fortunately, she was very helpful and understanding, telling us that the hot summer had seen the nit population explode and sales of the special shampoo they needed going through the roof.

She talked me through how to use the product and I raced back to the caravan site so we could all get relief as quickly as possible. We went over to the shower block in relays in a bid to avoid suspicion. Terry was the last to wash and finally we could all stop scratching.

Although we'd booked in for two weeks, at the end of the first, the heavens opened and it poured down with rain. 'That's why it's called the Lake District,' Terry laughed, trying to put a brave face on it, but the weather got all of us down. We finally admitted defeat on the Sunday, packed up and went home.

'This is absolutely, positively my very last caravan holiday!' I declared on the way home and I wasn't the only one to feel that way.

Chapter Seventeen

Sharon was eleven years old when she came to live with us and it was less than a month before things took a turn for the worst.

We assigned her the spare fourth bedroom and I set to work decorating it especially for her. You'd think that Terry would have been grateful, but instead my efforts served only to cause friction. He came in to inspect my work when I was about halfway through and immediately started picking fault, telling me that I wasn't doing my best for Sharon. Incensed at the accusation, I downed tools and told him that he'd better do the job himself, then. Of course he didn't, so the room stayed unfinished until he finally apologised.

I wasn't to know it then, but this was to be his attitude towards me as far as his girls were concerned. No matter how hard I tried, I was not doing enough.

There was another unforeseen problem with the new set up. Whereas Nicola, Sophie and I had all gotten along perfectly well together, the arrival of Sharon in our midst upset the balance of the family. Before the swap, Nicola had always lived in her sister's shadow, there being no doubt as to who was the favourite with her parents. Thus Nicola had enjoyed living with Sophie since I treated them both equally, buying them the same clothes and toys. Sharon living with Rita meant that Nicola could also enjoy the affection of her father without having to compete for his attention with her older sister.

Sharon moving in changed all that, and battle recommenced between Nicola and her sister, the younger girl determined not to be outdone by Sharon. Never the tidiest of children at the best of times, Nicola had always tried to please me and do her best to maintain a modicum of tidiness. When Sharon came to stay, all that went out the window. Sharon kept an untidy room, so Nicola did the same, vying to be the centre of attention.

To me, Sharon's behaviour seemed to be a form of rebellion, or silent defiance as I called it. However, if I dared to complain to Terry about the state of his girls' bedrooms, his response was always 'if you don't like it, don't go in there.' I didn't have to clear up after my own daughter so there was no way I was going to do so for my stepdaughters. I only wanted them to keep their rooms tidy, not spring clean them. Was that too much to ask?

~

Summer 1978 brought yet another twist to the stresses and strains that had plagued me since remarrying. Since Rita had failed to effectively parent Sharon, she turned her attention to Nicola and started filling her head with new ideas. This was immediately apparent to me after her return from a trip to Derbyshire.

Sophie hadn't gone with the other children, begging me not to send her, so she'd enjoyed a holiday with her granny by the seaside. Perhaps if she'd been with the girls, she'd have been able to tell me what had happened. Still, I could see that Nicola was unhappy when we collected her from Rita's mother's flat in London.

We had always co-ordinated things so that when the children went to stay up North, we took them to their granny in London so that Robert could collect them for the second half of the journey. When we picked up Sharon and Nicola, I asked Nicola what was wrong.

'Nothing,' came the sulky reply, 'but I'm not going to call you Mum any more. You're not my Mum and I don't know why I have to call you that.'

'That's okay, Nicola,' I replied calmly, 'I've never made you call me Mum. You can call me Kathy if you want to.' She had no idea that I was feeling terrible inside. After looking after her for six years, seeing her off to school, treating her as if she were my own, now she'd decided things should be different.

It was clear that this wasn't an idea that had originated with Nicola and I sensed Rita's involvement. Sophie confirmed my suspicions when she told me that Nicola had said she wanted to live with her Mum.

Worried, I tried to talk about it with Terry, but he waved my concerns away, telling me not to take any notice. And why should he be bothered? He had what he'd wanted all along: both of his daughters under his roof.

However, the problem wouldn't go away and the more I tried to talk to him about it, the more we argued. Terry would never listen to my side of the story, always taking his girls' side against me.

One particular moment sticks in my mind when Terry's parents came round for dinner. I'd gone out of my way to prepare all their favourite dishes, but when I brought out my prized lemon meringue pie, Sharon turned her nose up at it, declaring 'this pastry's stale.'

'That's funny. I had no complaints about my cooking before you came to stay with us,' I retorted angrily.

'It's all right, Sharon,' Terry said. 'Kathy can't take criticism.'

I left the room seething with anger, feeling totally humiliated. If it had been an isolated incident, perhaps I would have handled it better, but it was just one of many and perfectly encapsulated the gradual undermining of my confidence as mistress of my home in the two years since Sharon had come to live with us.

Without realising it, I was gradually becoming depressed and unsure of myself. Everything came to a head one evening while I was at my weekly Weightwatchers class. I'd struck up a friendship with a fellow Weightwatcher, Sheila. When it was my turn to be weighed, the leader announced 'only half a pound loss this week, Mrs Farmer,' making me feel that once more, my efforts weren't good enough.

I burst into tears, much to the consternation of the group and my embarrassment. Sheila took me to one side, offering me tissues and realising instantly that my emotional outburst had nothing to do with my weight loss. As it turned out, she only lived a few minutes away by car, so she invited me round to hers the next morning for coffee.

When she invited me in, it wasn't long before I was pouring my heart out to her. She was so easy to talk to that I felt as though I'd known her all my life. She understood exactly what I was going through because she was also on her second marriage due to exactly the same set of circumstances. Incredibly, she'd swapped her husband for the next door neighbour's.

We compared notes and discovered that we had a lot in common. No wonder she'd been able to be so supportive the night before. Sheila proved a great comfort to me over the next twelve years until her premature death at the age of fifty.

Sharon went to the same comprehensive school as Sheila's daughter, Michelle, and the pair were even in the same class. Coincidentally, their birthdays were only one day apart, giving the girls a connection. Sharon and Michelle spent a lot of time together, giving Sheila and I the opportunity to do the same.

I was now bitterly regretting ever having agreed to let Sharon into our home. I'd tried to discuss my concerns with Terry, but to no avail. He wouldn't hear a word said against his daughter. I was at my wits' end. My health was deteriorating, my work suffering and I couldn't stop crying, so I went to see my doctor. He prescribed Valium, but diagnosed the issues with my stepdaughters as the real cause of my illness and state of mind, confirming what I already suspected.

~

Christmas 1978 was approaching and it was agreed that Sharon and Nicola could spend it in Derbyshire with their 'other' family. Sophie was to stay with us and we went to spend Christmas with my parents in Thanet.

Now that I was away from Terry's girls, I felt as though a weight had been lifted from my shoulders. My mother, noticing that I wasn't myself asked what was wrong.

Once I started to talk, I couldn't stop and everything came pouring out, my problems with Sharon, Nicola's change of attitude, Terry's complete refusal to support me and the constant put downs and undermining of my confidence.

'I'm worried about you,' my mother told me. 'If things don't change, your heath *and* your sanity will suffer. Can't you talk to Terry about all this?'

'I've tried,' I wailed. 'It's no good trying to reason with him. He won't listen. I'd have to do something drastic to make him see sense.'

'What do you mean by drastic?'

In that moment, I knew what I needed to do. 'I'll have to leave him. I can't go on like this.'

'How will you manage?' asked my mother.'

'Can I come back home with you for the moment?' I pleaded. 'Just while I get back on my feet again.'

'Of course you can, but when? And how will you manage it all?'

I had no idea, but together, Mum and I hatched a plan of action. When Terry and I went home after the Christmas break, Sophie would stay at her grandparents while I tried one last time to make Terry see sense. If I couldn't get Terry to agree to send Sharon back to her mother, then I'd leave him and join Sophie at my parents.

When I explained my intentions to Sophie, any concerns I had that she might be upset at the prospect of moving out were unfounded.

'About time!' she grinned.

I had everything planned. One way or another, Terry was going to listen to me.

Chapter Eighteen

Leaving Sophie with my parents for the time being, I chose my moment carefully to talk to Terry. When the two of us were alone, I sat down with him over a cup of tea, took a deep breath and began.

'Things aren't working out,' I said gently.

'What do you mean?'

'I can't cope with all three of the girls. Sharon needs to go back to Rita.'

The second I said it, I knew what his reaction would be. Terry erupted.

'Absolutely no way!' he raged. 'You know what it's taken to get both my girls here, how hard it's been for us all to be separated. You want to undo all of that and send Sharon away? Out of the question!'

'But can't you see I can't cope?' I pointed out. 'I've done my best. She's been here for two years. Nobody can say we haven't tried, but it's just not working.'

'Then you'll just have to try harder,' Terry shrugged. 'Sharon's staying and that's the end of it.'

'Don't you get it? If you don't listen to me, this could be the end of us.' I was starting to lose my temper.

'You won't be going anywhere,' Terry replied confidently.

'So my feelings don't count and I just have to get on with our family life and make the best of it?'

'If that's how you want to see it.' Terry left the room, our conversation at an end.

I resolved there and then to put my plan into action and leave him before I lost my mind and had a breakdown. I could feel myself heading towards a complete nervous collapse and had no intention of putting myself through that.

~

Terry was on an early shift and he returned to work on Saturday morning, leaving me to my own devices until two o'clock. I was supposed to pick him up from work and then we'd travel up together to London to collect the girls, but I just couldn't face the two of them again.

I rang my mother and told her that I would be catching the next available train to Westwood Station. She told me that my father had suggested that I leave a letter for Terry explaining everything just in case he called the police and reported me missing.

I sat down and scribbled out a short note.

Terry,

I'm sorry, but I simply can't cope any more. I've done my best, but Sharon being here is making things impossible. Until the situation is resolved and she returns to live with her mother, I won't be coming back.

Much as I hate to do this, there really is no other option and you need to choose: your wife or your daughter.

Kathy

Leaving the note propped up in front of the kettle where Terry was bound to see it, I raced out to Sheila's car and she drove me to the station. I caught the first available train and was safely in Thanet by mid-morning. Once I got to Mum's I phoned Terry's work, leaving a message telling him that I couldn't pick him up so he'd need to make alternative arrangements.

Having made the break and being back home with my family, I felt a huge sense of relief, but my happiness was tempered by my fear of Terry's reaction. He was hot tempered, used to arguing forcefully to get his own way. It was his verbal bullying that had led to my leaving, but I worried what it would mean for my escape.

'Come on Kathy. Let's get down to the shops to pick up a few bits and bobs,' Mum suggested and Sophie and I pulled on our coats, wanting the chance to do something. It had snowed and the air was fresh, but the corner shop wasn't far and once we reached it, I let Sophie pick out some sweets as a small compensation for all the upheaval.

Gingerly picking our way along the snow covered pavement to get back, my mother asked 'what time do you think you will hear from him?'

I thought for a moment. 'He doesn't finish work until two o'clock and then he will have to get home and find the letter, so I suppose we are safe until around four,' I replied.

Just as the words passed my lips, we heard a car skid to a halt on the icy road, pulling up beside us. Sophie screamed and I looked up to see Terry with an expression on his face as black as thunder.

I shall never forget that angry, evil looking face staring through the windscreen as long as I live. Fortunately, we were just going past a friend's house, so Sophie ran to safety, closely followed by my mother. She quickly explained the situation and asked the friends to mind Sophie and call my brother, instructing him to drive round as if he were just popping by for a visit.

Terry leapt out of the car, yelling at me. 'Get in! You're coming home with me!'

I shook my head, hiding my fear. 'No. Not until you sort out the question of the children.'

Terry wasn't even listening, acting like a madman with staring eyes. He stormed over and grabbed hold of my arm, trying to pull me towards the car, but I clung on to the railings of a nearby house and held tight.

My mother had come out of the house and pleaded with Terry to leave me alone. 'Can't you see she's in no fit state to go anywhere?'

What a sight we must have made to anyone watching in this quiet, top-of-the-market, millionaire's road.

Terry seemed to calm down a little. 'Alright, then. Get into the car and I'll take you back to your mother's. We can talk there.'

'It's all right. I'd rather walk,' I told him. 'It's only a few yards round the corner. I can manage.' I had a sneaky suspicion that if I got into the car, he'd whisk me back to our house and I had no intention of going anywhere with him.

Realising I wouldn't be tricked, Terry got back into the car and drove the very short distance back to my mother's, leaving us to walk.

'Don't let him talk you into going back if you don't want to,' Mum advised as we reached her front door.

Terry followed us in and stood menacingly over me as I sat at the kitchen table. Mum bustled about, making a cup of tea, but Terry ignored all her attempts at small talk, glaring at me menacingly without saying a word.

At last, he broke the silence. 'Come on, Kathy. How can we talk properly if we're not alone? At least give me a chance to put things right. You owe me that much at least.'

At that moment, Tony, my oldest brother, popped his head round the back door. 'Hello, Terry! Fancy seeing you here! How are you doing?' Tony later told me that he was very scared of Terry and had taken the precaution of looking in his car boot before he came in to check that he hadn't brought his shotgun with him. Terry must have sensed Tony's agitation because he ignored my brother, saying to me 'I'm taking you back home with me and *he's* not going to stop me.'

I sighed. 'All right. Let's go upstairs to talk.' I couldn't allow any more arguments in my mother's home and I certainly didn't want to risk Terry lashing out at Tony. My brother was bound to come offworse in any fist fight. If my father had been there, perhaps things might have been different – Terry had always respected him – but he was in London all day for a business meeting.

Alone in the bedroom, Terry turned on the charm, assuring me that if I went home with him now, he'd make sure that Sharon would behave herself. 'Just give me thirteen weeks to Easter and if you still feel the same way, I'll take her back to her mother's myself,' he promised.

'It's already too late.' I shook my head. 'She could be a perfect little angel for the next three months, but I still want her to go back.'

'Come on, Kathy. Be reasonable. She's just a child. I know things can work out if you just give her a chance.'

'I've already given her plenty of chances,' I pointed out. 'The pair of you have worn me down and Nicola's not helped either. With Sharon gone, we might just be able to return to normality.'

'It's not long until Easter,' countered Terry. 'Now that I can see how upset you are, I'll make sure that things will be different. You'll see. We'll make it work. I promise.'

I had serious doubts that this was true, but I was too tired to fight any more and agreed to go home with him, if for no other reason than the fact that I felt my family had suffered enough for one day. At least he'd seen that I meant business and maybe he would stick to his word and change after all.

I gathered up the few possessions I'd brought with me and we went round to pick up Sophie before going home. As soon as we arrived, he set off for London to collect his girls, having phoned ahead to say he had been delayed. Time would tell whether he would keep his promises.

Chapter Nineteen

I've always believed that trial separations don't work. If a relationship has broken down to the extent that one partner leaves home, it's already too late and the marriage is doomed, no matter how hard people try. So it was in our case.

Sharon and Nicola returned home, thirteen weeks flew past and it was Easter. Sharon and Nicola went up to Derbyshire for the holidays and I was determined that only one girl would come back. Three months hadn't changed my mind about Sharon. Her behaviour had been quite acceptable initially, but despite my best efforts trying to manage with three daughters, it was no use, and as the time came for them to return, I was getting in a real mess, knowing that Terry would hit the roof when I insisted that Sharon stay with her mother.

I had considered an alternative. By now, Nicola was keen to stay with her Mum and I thought that it might make more sense for her to go instead of Sharon, since she actively wanted to stay there. My personal preference was for Sharon to leave, but one less child to care for would be a step in the right direction and possibly less stressful.

The girls were due back in a fortnight and as the days passed, it became clear that Terry wasn't interested in discussing the situation. In a moment of madness, I decided to phone Rita and propose my plan that Nicola have some time with her Mum. Rita told me she'd talk to Robert and call back. I knew that I'd need to pick my moment carefully to talk about my idea with Terry, but Rita rang sooner than expected and Terry answered the phone.

Panicking, I locked myself in the downstairs toilet. My stomach was churning and I was shaking all over.

I heard Terry end the call and suddenly footsteps headed my way. I shrieked as there was a bang on the door. Terry was punching and kicking at it, shouting for me to come out. I had no choice but to face the music or deal with a shattered door.

I emerged to face a raging bull and the row to end all rows exploded. For once, I wouldn't let Terry bulldoze me and I made it quite clear that our marriage was at an end. I simply wasn't going to be a skivvy to his girls and accept Sharon's insolent attitude.

Perhaps Terry recognised that I really did mean it and all the shouting in the world wouldn't change anything, so he finally agreed to let Nicola stay with her mother. I packed up her things and Terry left for Derbyshire to bring back Sharon.

Watching his car pull away, I was full of conflicting emotions. I was very fond of Nicola. She'd been living with us for seven years and I'd grown close to her in that time. I was also worried about how this change would affect living with Terry after his big sacrifice. Would yet another upheaval denote happier, stress free times for us all? I suspected not and as the year wore on, summer time saw no improvement in my situation.

Sharon became more and more defiant. She'd inherited her father's temper and way with words and after one particularly nasty row with her, I arrived at work, suffered a serious nose bleed and burst into floods of tears. I was in no fit state to do anything and one of my colleagues kindly took me home.

All this fuss over the state of Sharon's room and the fact that I had failed to make her bed that morning.

There was no point in turning to Terry for support. Despite his promises that things would change, Sharon could do no wrong in his eyes. What was worse, Sheila told me that Michelle had said that Sharon was playing truant. I rang the school who confirmed that there was a problem with Sharon's attendance. I knew there would be no point in my trying to talk to Terry about his precious daughter, so I asked the school to send him a letter telling him about her behaviour. He wouldn't be able to ignore that, I reasoned.

However, Sharon wasn't the only problem we had. Since I'd left for that one day at Christmas, Terry had become very possessive, wanting to know my every move. Things came to a head one Friday evening when I agreed to go shopping with Sheila out of town without telling him first. Sophie was at a friend's for tea and Sharon was off with her crowd, so I took the opportunity to have a few hours' respite with Sheila. We had such a good time that we decided to extend our day with dinner, making me that little bit later coming home.

As soon as I walked through the door, I was hit with a barrage of verbal abuse. How *dare* I go shopping without him!

As Terry ranted and raved, my thoughts wandered to the possibility of leaving. I didn't love him any more, was afraid of him, even, and I was tired of the constant strain of trying to make sure I didn't put a foot wrong or face his wrath.

After he left for work on Saturday, I phoned my mother and asked again if I could stay with her. By this time, I was really run down, the constant rows having taken their toll on my health. I had an abscess on my tooth and a boil on my neck. I looked and felt awful and the only thing that got me through the day was Valium.

I had an appointment on the following Monday to have the tooth removed and we agreed that my parents would come and pick me up from home on Monday morning after Terry had left for work and the girls were safely at school. I swore Sophie to secrecy and told her to be ready to leave school in the morning. She sorted out a few things she wanted to take and piled them in her bedroom. Seeing the excitement and happiness on Sophie's face that this nightmare would soon be over was all the reassurance I needed that I'd made the right decision.

First there was the weekend to get through. On Sunday, we'd arranged to go on a boat trip with another couple, George and Diane, leaving from the Medway Towns and going over the Medway River to Southend. Sophie came with us but Sharon chose to stay home and spend the day with her friends.

Nobody could miss the fact that something was seriously wrong with me. I looked terrible and Diane took me to one side. 'What's wrong?' she asked.

Too emotional to keep the secret, I told her my plans. 'I'm leaving Terry,' I whispered. 'Tomorrow morning, if I can get away. Please don't tell him. Please.'

Diane was shocked but assured me that my secret was safe with her, seeing just how bad things were between us.

I couldn't enjoy the day. Not only was I worried about the next day, I didn't like being at sea at the best of times and I was so glad when it was over and we were back on dry land heading home.

Things went from bad to worse, however, when we arrived to discover the contents of my handbag strewn across the garden. One of our back windows had been smashed and our house burgled.

'You'd better call the police,' ordered Terry, as he went to check over the house.

The detectives were soon on the scene to do what they could, but as they left, they warned us that there wasn't much hope of recovering the stolen money and cards.

I began to panic; this just one more thing to add to the list of complications I couldn't deal with. Supposing the detectives wanted to come back on Monday? Supposing Terry took the day off work to speak to them? I had to get a message to my Dad to wait until the coast was clear, but how could I do that with Terry watching my every move?

'You'd better go round to next door to see if they saw or heard anything,' ordered Terry. For once, I let his controlling nature wash over me, seeing the opportunity to make a phone call. Once next door, I told my neighbours everything. They were very understanding and not at all judgemental. They'd probably heard our arguments after all. They let me use their phone and I was able to warn my parents not to leave Thanet until I told them it was safe with Terry and work and the girls at school.

I was so terrified that something might happen to spoil my plans that I lay in bed that night, shaking with fear that Terry might suspect something was up. He always seemed to know what was on my mind when I was upset.

'What's the matter with you?' he asked irritably.

Oh my God, he suspects!

'You're only going to have a tooth out, for goodness' sake.'

He thinks I'm shaking because of the dentist. Thank goodness.

‘Well I haven’t had a tooth out for about twenty years,’ I replied as calmly as possible.

‘You’ll be all right. You’re having the day off to get over it. Some of us have got to go to work you know.’

What a relief. I think I’ll be able to get away after all.

~

The next morning, Terry went to work for his six o’clock shift. Sharon and Sophie left for school and I gathered together clothes and toiletries, as well as Sophie’s belongings.

Once again, I left a note, and when my escape committee arrived at eleven o’clock, we quickly loaded up the car. I climbed in the back and lay flat across the back seat so no one would see me. We weren’t taking any chances.

We collected Sophie from school and headed off to London to stay with my favourite Aunt, safely out of harm’s way where Terry would never find us. Once we arrived, there was one final chore to take care of. I called work and asked that my salary not be paid into our joint account any more. They agreed to keep it on hold until I’d opened my own bank account.

Away again and at last I felt that wonderful feeling of relief at being away from my tyrant of a husband.

Chapter Twenty

My Auntie welcomed us with open arms. Sophie and I were both absolutely shattered but so pleased to be free of Terry and Sharon.

Mum and Dad stayed just long enough to see us settled in before they left to go back to Thanet and as I waved them away, I fought off a sense of foreboding at Terry's reaction when he discovered me gone.

Everything was looking up, except for the pain from my tooth. Fortunately, my cousin Carole worked as a dental technician in Fulham and was able to squeeze me in as an emergency. I went with her the next morning and had the tooth extracted. If only all my problems were so easily solved.

I stayed in London for a week and those seven days were the happiest we'd enjoyed for a while. My Auntie spoilt us rotten and during the day I enjoyed watching the tennis at Wimbledon on the television. Sophie visited the nearby park and some shops, but although I knew she was old enough to take care of herself, I couldn't completely rid myself of the fear that Terry would come roaring up in his Jaguar to take us away. He knew about my Aunt but didn't know her address and he phoned my mother, hassling her to tell him my whereabouts. She stood firm and didn't tell him anything, but I subsequently found out from Sheila that Terry had been threatening to go down to Thanet with his shotgun to force my father to tell him where I was staying, a terrifying thought.

When the week was up, feeling refreshed and rested, having recovered from the tooth extraction, I went back to Thanet to my parents to make some plans for my future. While I was there, Terry's friend Richard phoned, claiming he needed to speak to me urgently. My mother told him I was out, but Richard persisted, saying it was a matter of life and death. My mother told him that she'd make sure I rang and after she hung up, Dad advised that I make the call from a public call box, just in case.

Richard answered after just one ring. 'I've just called in to see Terry and found him unconscious on the floor. What are you going to do about it?'

'What do you mean, what am I going to do about it? What have *you* done about it?'

Richard's reaction told me everything I needed to know about the reality of the situation. 'What? Oh, er, I've called an ambulance.'

I laughed bitterly. 'Really?'

'Look, you have to come back home,' Richard urged. 'Your husband needs you. Doesn't your marriage mean anything to you?'

'I'm sorry, Richard. I'm not going to talk about this with you.' I hung up. I had a strong suspicion that Terry wasn't in any danger and this was just a ruse to get me back home. I refused to be drawn into his little games.

When drama didn't work, Terry came down to Thanet in person, begging me to come back. Seeing him sitting in my parents' lounge sobbing his eyes out didn't move me and I stayed firm in my resolve to stay where I was.

Now that I'd faced my demons, I felt strong enough to go back to work. I couldn't stay away much longer or I'd lose my job and I'd need every penny to support me and Sophie. Since it was the school holidays, Sophie stayed with my mother during the day so I could go back to my secretarial duties. I loved being back at work and my colleagues were equally pleased to see me. At last it felt as though life could go back to normal.

The only downside was that Terry worked quite close to me and I knew it was only a matter of time before he sought me out. Sure enough, one lunch time I found him waiting for me at the gate. He pleaded with me to go and have lunch and promised that's all it would be: a simple meal with no pressure.

I knew this wasn't going to be the case and once we had our food, Terry immediately started talking about how things would be different if I went back. I stopped him dead in his tracks, pointing out that there wasn't enough time to discuss everything during our lunch break. I promised I'd have dinner with him for my birthday the following week, a promise that satisfied him for the time being. Once more, I had some peace from my troubled marriage.

~

My birthday approached and my father was dead against my seeing Terry. He warned me that it would be a mistake to let him talk me round again, seeing that I was beginning to soften a little now that I'd had a break.

The problem was the practical side of things. I couldn't see how I could survive as a single parent and couldn't face the prospect of a second divorce with all that entailed, especially since I didn't think that it would be nearly as amicable with Terry. Throughout it all, my boss had been very understanding and suggested that I might be able to rent a property in town from one of our directors. I put my name down for the first available apartment, but nothing would be available for a while. I'd just have to wait.

My 39th birthday dawned and after an uneventful day at work, I went over to Sheila's to get ready for my birthday treat.

'Terry's been on at me ever since you left,' she told me. 'He comes round at all hours wanting to know where you are and how you're doing. The man's a mess. What are you going to tell him tonight?'

'I don't know.' It was true. I hadn't made up my mind one way or another, much as I wanted to escape. As soon as I'd left Terry this time, he'd promptly sent Sharon to live with her mother, a step in the right direction since she'd been the source of many of the problems in our marriage.

'Are you sure you really want to end things?' Sheila went on. 'You could lose so much.'

'I do wonder what things will be like without Sharon,' I replied, but before we could talk about things in any depth, Terry was at the door and we left for our meal.

Surprisingly, it was a wonderful evening, just like old times. Of course, Terry continued to beg me to go home. He promised that I'd never have to look after his girls again and told me that he realised that he had to make a choice and he chose me. He knew that the girls were best off with their mother and he'd been wrong to treat me the way he did.

Pretty words, but would he keep his promises?

As Terry talked, I could feel myself relenting, wondering what life would be like if it was just the three of us, Terry, Sophie and me. I'd worked very hard to build our house and create a good life for us all.

Some time back in the spring I'd booked a holiday for myself on a pottery course in Wiltshire. I was going to the renowned Marlborough College which opened its doors during the summer holidays to students wanting to pursue artistic subjects. Terry had agreed to let me go in return for my allowing him to buy a boat we really couldn't afford. By the end of the evening, I found myself agreeing to give our marriage one last try, but not until after my holiday.

There was one major condition to my return: the girls would never stay with us again. If Terry wanted to see them, I would go and stay with my mother during their visit if necessary. He was more than welcome to go on holiday with his daughters and I'd happily miss out on the trip if it meant I wouldn't have to be with them.

Terry happily agreed to everything I said, just wanting me back home. Once again, his silver tongue had talked me round and once again, I would live to regret my decision.

Sophie was very unhappy with my news. She would have much preferred to stay with her grandparents, but I had my pottery break and Terry came to pick me up afterwards. We spent Saturday night together at home before going to Thanet to collect Sophie the next morning.

I'll never forget my father's parting words: 'I give you six weeks, and you will wish that you had never returned home.'

Chapter Twenty One

So it was that I was back home again for a second attempt at wedded bliss, this time without Sharon. This should have been the perfect solution, life with just the three of us. The house seemed empty without the other girls and incredibly tidy.

Terry tried his best to go on without his daughters and at first all was well. However, it didn't take long before little cracks started to appear and arguments once more became a feature of our daily life.

Terry had bought a second hand dog kennel he needed to take up to Derbyshire. Rita and Robert had bought Nicola a puppy and Sophie asked if she could go with him to visit John. Terry was glad of the company and the pair made plans to be away for the weekend. Left to my own devices, I decided to go and see my parents.

I waved goodbye to Terry and Sophie on Friday evening and took the train to Thanet the next morning. My mother was especially pleased to see me because she'd just heard the sad news that my grandmother had passed away. I was glad to be able to be there to comfort her through her grief and stayed longer than I'd originally planned so I could offer her support. I didn't even think about Terry on his way back from Derbyshire. It wasn't important given what had just happened. He was a grown man and could look after himself.

It turned out I was wrong about that. The phone rang late in the afternoon. I picked it up and was happy to hear Sheila's voice.

'I've got Terry here. He wants to speak to you,' she told me.

'Why isn't he calling from home?' I asked, a puzzled frown wrinkling my forehead.

'He's locked himself out,' Shelia explained, passing the phone over to my husband.

'Why aren't you here?' demanded Terry. 'I came home and you weren't there.'

There it was, that tone of voice I knew all too well, sending a shiver of fear down my spine. I could just imagine the irate expression on his face. Still, I kept my voice calm, not wanting to anger him any further.

'I've stayed a bit longer because my granny died yesterday and my mum is very upset,' I replied.

'So what train will you be on then?' Typical Terry, completely ignoring the fact that I was going through a bereavement. 'I need you back home as soon as possible.'

I sighed. 'I'll get the next train,' I told him. It arrives in Chatham at seven thirty.'

'I'll be waiting.' With those threatening words, Terry hung up without saying goodbye.

My father drove me to the train station and on the drive, I quietly admitted to him that his words to me the last time I'd left had been sadly true. I realised what a mistake it had been to try to save my marriage and this really hit home when Terry met me at the station. Without preamble, he said to me, 'You don't give a fuck for no one, do you?'

'It's not my fault you forgot your key,' I countered bravely. 'How terrible of me to stay at my Mum's for two whole days when she's just lost someone.'

'Selfish bitch,' spat Terry, but I wouldn't be drawn into an argument and journeyed home in silence, angering him even more. How could I ever have thought that our life together would work out?

It wasn't just me who was miserable. I could see that Sophie was very unhappy after her visit to Derbyshire. Although she jumped at the opportunity to see her brother, life with the Andrews wasn't pleasant for her. Robert ignored her while Rita picked on her, taking out her frustrations at having both her girls back no doubt.

However, it wasn't as though things were any better with Terry and me. We fought constantly, Terry accusing me of putting the dog down unnecessarily and throwing his daughters out of the house. Far from life getting better with just the three of us, it was getting worse.

After one particularly tempestuous night when we'd argued well into the small hours, I lay awake in bed, asking myself "*What am I doing here with him? I don't love him. I despise him. Why did I ever agree to come back?*"

Although I tried my hardest to keep my emotions in check at work, it all became too much and I finally broke down in tears one morning in front of my boss.

'Things not going too well, lass?' he asked gently.

'No,' I sobbed. 'My father was right. I bitterly regret giving it another try.'

To make matters worse, just when I'd decided to go back to Terry, my name had reached the top of the waiting list for one of the flats the company rented out. I'd had to let it go, much to my embarrassment after all the effort my employers had gone to in order to make one available at short notice. When I'd apologised to the Docks Manager, he was very understanding, appreciating my decision to give it another go. As a local Justice of the Peace, he said he saw too many couples in court before him who gave up too easily on their marriage. Now my boss advised me to put my name down once again.

Once more I made the decision to leave, this time for good. However, now that I was really serious about saying goodbye to Terry, I wanted to be more prepared so I could do the job properly with no going back. I put my name on the waiting list but also kept my eye on the local newspaper for any available flats to let. I had replies sent to my mother's address so that Terry wouldn't know about my planned departure.

At the end of November, Terry and I went to the annual dinner and dance for my father's Masonic Lodge. Sophie went to some friends for the weekend and Terry and I headed over to Thanet. My parents' fortieth wedding anniversary was in December so they'd invited lots of family members to the dance to turn it into a real celebration.

Terry was a complete and utter pig the whole night, drinking too much and making loud, rude comments. When my mother secretly asked me how things were, she wasn't surprised to hear about my plans. 'Do you think you could wait until after Christmas before leaving?' she asked. 'I don't think I could cope with Terry bursting in, crying his eyes out and spoiling everyone's Christmas.'

'Of course, Mum.' I didn't want to make her suffer any more than I already had, but I wasn't sure whether I'd be able to keep the promise. Still, the chances were high that I wouldn't be able to find a flat for some months and I thought that I could hold on for that long.

As it turned out, the end came quite unexpectedly and wasn't planned at all.

Chapter Twenty Two

Just one week after the dance, Terry and I were in bed where all our rows took place. Yet again, we started arguing for what would turn out to be the last time.

'I can't do this anymore,' I told him frankly. 'I won't be staying with you forever. I'm looking into ways to end our relationship.'

'Just say you love me,' Terry demanded.

'But I don't, and I can't tell a lie about something so important.'

'Just say you love me,' he persisted.

Wearily, I said in a monotone 'I love you.'

'There you are,' he remarked smugly. 'That's not so bad. Now try to live up to it.'

I laughed ironically. 'It's not that simple and you know it.'

'So you're going to leave me one day, then?'

'Yes.'

'All right. Well if that's how It's going to be, if you're not going to work at our marriage, I won't work hard either,' Terry declared. 'No more overtime for me and if we can't manage financially, we'll just have to start selling some of your precious pots and jewellery. Your clutter takes up too much space anyway.'

My hobby was collecting antique pottery and over the past twenty years, I'd built up quite a valuable collection that was held in a showcase in the lounge. I knew exactly what Terry was saying. He'd lived in debt for most of his adult life before he met me and it wouldn't bother him one bit to live that way again. Knowing how I felt about living within our means, if he thought this would change my mind, he was mistaken. His threats just served as a reminder as to why I needed to go and strengthened my resolve.

Terry was on early shifts again and started work at six o'clock. Instead of taking his moped as he usually did, he dragged me out of bed to take him in the car. The roads were icy and Terry insisted on driving.

We reached a section of the road which had parked vehicles all down the left hand side, making it difficult for two cars to pass. Terry pulled out to drive in one direction, when I saw that there was a bus coming the other way. 'Stop Terry,' I warned, since the bus had right of way, but Terry kept going. I'll never forget the driver's face, staring out from his cab in fear and amazement as Terry careered towards him.

If Terry was hoping to frighten me into thinking he was going to crash the car, possibly killing both of us, he was sadly mistaken. I was scared, but I knew only too well he was too much of a coward to go through with it. I sat appearing calm on the outside, but shaking inside. He finally pulled up and moved in to let the bus pass.

A few minutes later we arrived outside his workplace. He got out, and as he left, I said under my breath, 'Good riddance.'

Safely at work, my Mum rang to let me know that a flat I'd enquired about had gone. Just my luck. I told her what had happened that morning and our argument the night before and she immediately advised me to get the pots out of the house and store them with a friend if possible. It made sense, and the way things were going, the sooner the better, so I asked my boss for a few hours off to go and deal with things.

I got some strong boxes from the basement that were used for storing old files and headed home to pack. Sheila had agreed to keep my things in her loft and she came out to help me unload.

'You do know that he's going to hit the roof when he gets home and sees all the pots gone,' she pointed out.

'I know,' I sighed. 'I don't think I can face any more rows. If I could, I'd go to my Mum's right now, but I don't think she'd have me.'

'Why don't you phone her and ask?' suggested Sheila. 'It can't do any harm.'

Sheila was right and I used her phone to call home. 'Mum, can I come home now please?' I begged. 'I can't take any more. I know you said wait until after Christmas, but I just don't think I can.'

Mum could hear the desperation in my voice. 'Okay,' she said. 'Come on home'.

On hearing the news, Sheila shot into action. 'You are not going empty handed,' she told me. 'We'll go right now and collect some more of your things before we get Sophie from school.'

We drove over to the house and I backed into the garage for an easy getaway. Working as quickly as we could, we threw my things into cases and black plastic bags, dumping them in the back of the car. I got as much of Sophie's belongings as I could and even took my homemade Christmas pudding. We were working in a small panic, terrified that Terry would somehow know what was going on and come back to stop us.

Unloading a second cargo, Sheila was ready to go back for a third load, but I put my foot down. 'I don't want to go back to that house. I'm too afraid.'

Taking just two cases of personal items, I drove to Sophie's school to collect her. It seemed to take an eternity for her to appear and she arrived carrying freshly baked mince pies from her cookery class.

Sophie was surprised to see me, but relieved to be going again, especially when I promised her that it was for good this time. We said our goodbyes to Sheila and headed for Chatham station to get to Thanet. I left the car at the train station and when we arrived at my mother's house, I phoned Terry's work and told his foreman where he could collect the car from.

Away from Terry and this time for good. No more going back. No more broken promises. No more nagging. No more arguments.

We stood on Chatham Station eating hot mince pies with the snow gently falling all around us. My nightmare was finally over and a new struggle was now facing me – surviving as a single Mum on a limited income with a malicious husband spreading rumours about me round the docks.

Chapter Twenty Three

I took a week off work to get settled in at Thanet. Sophie missed a few days of school, but we both got back into our normal routines as quickly as possible. Sheila rang me to say that Terry had been round to her house and she'd told him that I'd left him for good. Terry seemed to accept that it was over between us and at last I could start to move on.

Sophie and I made the trek to Medway Towns every weekday, her to go to school, me to get to work. It was expensive and time consuming but it was worth it for the relief we felt at being free from Terry.

Despite my mother's fears that Terry would ruin everything, we had a lovely relaxing Christmas with my Mum and Dad and in the New Year, I received notice that a flat was available for me in town. The Dock Manager's wife was to be my new landlady and I took possession of my new flat on 8th February.

Immediately I set to work transforming it into a home for me and Sophie. It was very dreary in its current state and when the last tenants removed their furniture and belongings, I could see just how much there was to do. Of course, money was tight. I only had my wages to support us, seventy seven pounds a week after tax and the flat cost me seventy pounds a month. Sophie was now a teenager and I was having to support two adults on that modest amount. Still, I didn't even think about asking Terry for financial help. I knew it would be a waste of time, even though Sophie became his responsibility when we got married so I could have claimed maintenance from him. I could also have turned to Robert for support, but I refused to apply to him either.

Keen to formalise things, I went to see a solicitor as soon as possible and applied for Legal Aid. I had to go through means testing and even on my limited income, I was assessed at being able to pay eleven pounds a month towards the cost of divorce. For the first time in my adult life, I was really hard up and struggling.

With the stress of it all, I lost weight and people thought I was joking when I said I couldn't afford to eat, but there was an element of truth in my words. Still, I managed to brighten up the flat with a couple of lucky bargains, including a deal with my landlady when she purchased a three piece suite from a colleague at work who had to clear out her mother's house after she died. I'd bought a cheap carpet on hire purchase for the lounge and I said I'd leave it when I moved out if I could use the furniture.

Another stroke of good fortune occurred on the day I moved in. Another colleague, Audrey, who went on to become my best friend, took me to her mother's flat in Maidstone for the same reason and told me to take anything I needed.

It was like being let loose in an Aladdin's cave. Linen, furniture, food in the cupboard, washing powder, electric fire, you name it, I found it. As I selected all the items, I frantically started calculating how I could pay for it all. Eventually I decided to offer a set amount per week until the debt was paid.

After loading up Audrey's van with my treasure, we went round to see her two brothers to negotiate a price for everything.

I couldn't believe my ears when they said 'how about five pounds for the lot?' I was overwhelmed with their kindness. It was an absolute life saver because the car load of effects I'd managed to get out of my house were lost when I spread them around the house. My mother had given me a few items, but my new 'home' was very humble indeed.

~

I'd instructed my solicitor to start divorce proceedings while I was still living at Thanet. Terry ignored all communications and my solicitor told me that he couldn't begin any action until Terry had been to a solicitor and acknowledged our letters.

I'd asked to be able to take certain items of furniture and personal effects as my share of the matrimonial home. I'd done my best to be fair and my list certainly didn't add up to half of the contents. Despite this, Terry totally ignored my request.

I was so angry I couldn't sleep at night. I needed many personal things for Sophie and me, not least of which was possession of the certificates of my qualifications from school and college. I never mentioned them in any of my letters because I knew that Terry would destroy them if he knew where they were and they were irreplaceable.

I decided to take drastic action. I knew that Terry had changed the locks on our house, so gaining entry was a problem. According to my solicitor, as long as my name was on the deeds, I couldn't be prosecuted for breaking into my on home. He stressed the importance of this point and I was most definitely on the deeds, but as Mrs Andrews, since we'd bought the land before my first divorce.

My plan was quite simple. I'd hire the biggest van you can drive with an ordinary licence, go to my old house, break in and take the things he wouldn't give me.

I booked a day's leave for when I thought Terry would be away at a meeting with his union. I also booked storage for my things, since I didn't yet have access to my flat. As a precaution, I called the local police station to ask for supervision while I went into my house. Terry had made it quite clear in his few communications with me that he would 'shoot my legs off' if I went anywhere near the house and I didn't want to take any risks. Fortunately they agreed, and told me that two constables would be outside the house, but wouldn't come in or intervene in any domestic matters.

I pulled up outside the house and tried unsuccessfully to reverse the van into our driveway, the presence of two policemen going some way towards making me feel self-conscious. Not used to driving a large van, I eventually gave up after several attempts and just drove in.

My partner in crime was my brother's girlfriend, Margot. She carried a crowbar under her jacket as we went round to the rear of the house. We used it to break open a small window and managed to open the back door into the dining room.

I suspected that Terry had arranged to have the house watched and was terrified that he'd come crashing through the door at any moment, so my first act was to hide his shotguns. I knew he kept them in the wardrobe, so I found them quite easily and put them under the mattress in his bed. Next I gathered up all my papers and put them safely in the van. Meanwhile, Margot was loading up the van as quickly as possible.

I joined her and we started moving the heavier pieces of furniture. We disconnected the washing machine ready to lift out, but before we could start moving it, the policemen on guard called me over to say they had to leave to attend a traffic incident.

'But what should I do if Terry appeared?' I asked in a panic.

'Just call 999 and they'll send someone,' they reassured me.

Yes, but how quickly will they arrive?

There was nothing I could do to get them to stay, so they left and we carried on loading.

Then I saw Terry driving hell for leather up the side road near our house on his way to get Richard, his great friend and collaborator in the 'attempted suicide' fiasco. There was no time to lose, so I went indoors and called the police as I'd been advised. 'Can you send someone please?' I begged. 'He's seen me and I'm sure he will be coming.' To my horror, I saw his car pull up behind my van on the drive. I watched him through the glass porch way. 'He's here, he's here! Please come quickly.'

With that, I put the phone down and stood for a few moments in the hall under the staircase to collect myself. Once I felt ready, I turned round and walked straight into his fist. Terry grabbed me and pushed me violently against the treads of the stairway, slamming my head against the hard wood. I fell to my knees and he started punching me. I remember thinking *how can I hurt him without needing much strength?*

As he reached for me, I grabbed his genitals and squeezed with all my might. Before he could retaliate, Margot came in from the kitchen door armed with the crowbar. 'The police are here Terry,' she told him. 'You'd better let her go.'

He went outside and started to unload my things from the van and dump them onto the front lawn. I saw Richard standing by the gateway and I yelled at him 'I don't know what you're doing here. It's none of your business.'

'I'm here as a friend to both of you. I'm trying to calm him down,' came the unconvincing reply.

By this time, the police were back. They waited a few moments and then asked if I was nearly ready to go. I would have been, but every time we put something on the van, Terry took something else off.

'Get your van off my drive!' he yelled.

'It's my drive as well and I'm entitled to be here,' I told him.

'Get your van off my drive!' he repeated.

'She can't go anywhere with your car parked in front of it,' pointed out one of the policemen, thus leading to the sweetest moment of the day.

Terry jumped into his car and in a fit of anger, reversed straight out, forgetting to close the door. I still remember the sound of the crunch as if it were yesterday. Music to my ears.

He had to drive forward again and close the door as best as he could before reversing out again. Margot defiantly loaded some last items from the lawn and we closed the doors. I decided that it was best to call it a day and not push my luck any further.

I asked the policemen to help me reverse my van out which they did, stopping the traffic to make life easier, and off I went with my precious load to the undertakers where I'd arranged to store my things. With everything safe among the coffins, we made our way back to Thanet with the empty van.

What an eventful and successful day. I'd faced up to my nemesis and got some of my stuff with the added bonus of seeing him destroy his car door. When relationships go sour and the love's gone, it is sad to admit that I got such enjoyment from his unfortunate accident.

Another unforeseen positive outcome was that after months of ignoring my solicitor's letters, Terry finally visited his brief and said he would sue me for the damage to the window as well as answer my petition for divorce. When my solicitor called me at work the next day to tell me the news, I replied that I'd countersue him for assault.

At last some action.

Chapter Twenty Four

With the bargains from Audrey's mum's estate and the deals I made with my landlady, it wasn't long before our flat became a cosy little nest for Sophie and me. The divorce was finally proceeding, but I knew that it would be a long and bitter battle.

My biggest fear was that I'd bump into Terry. My friends gave me regular updates on his whereabouts and one particular incident was particularly significant.

Going back to work after the Whitsun break, Audrey commented that she'd seen Terry driving into Chatham with a blonde woman and his car loaded up with what looked like household effects. I realised that the blonde woman was probably Margot, my brother's now ex-girlfriend, and the car was probably filled with items from my brother's house in Thanet.

Margot had mentioned to my mother that Terry had visited her to collect a squash racquet my brother had borrowed some time before. She'd said that she was scared of Terry and not happy that he'd come round. My brother was working in the Middle East at the time and had sadly decided to end his relationship with Margot. At the same time, he'd told her that he was quite happy to maintain his house in Thanet for as long as she needed and support her financially.

I phoned my mum to tell her what Audrey had said and she went straight round to my brother's house. The curtains were drawn, but there was a gap in the back kitchen curtains through which she could see that certain electrical items were missing. There was a big black hole where the oven once stood. Margot had obviously left the two cats to fend for themselves for the Whitsun weekend, as mum could hear them crying and scratching to get out of the house. She phoned me and confirmed my suspicions. Margot was moving into my house with Terry and the divorce hadn't yet been finally settled.

On another occasion, Sheila rang to say that she'd seen Terry driving out of Chatham in a truck, heading towards the coast road. Mum and Dad went round to my brother's house and parked at the end of the road to await developments. Sure enough, an hour later, Terry and Margot pulled up and started to load more household goods onto the truck.

My mother approached Margot and, totally ignoring Terry, said 'you are off then Margot?'

'Yes' she replied. 'I think it is what Edward wants.'

My parents stood waiting patiently, silently, while they loaded up the truck, then gave the house keys to my mother, driving off into the distance.

When my mother finally entered the house, it was in a disgusting state after the cats had been shut up for the long weekend. She phoned me later in tears and I promised to go down the next day and help her clear up the house.

~

That evening after finishing work, I went round to my old house to confront Terry about the new situation.

'Is Margot now living with you?' I demanded when he opened the door.

‘What does it matter to you?’ he asked.

‘Is Margot living with you?’ I repeated.

‘Yes, she’s staying here,’ came the reply.

‘That’s all I needed to know.’ I turned to walk back to my car, parked over the road, Terry following me.

‘Don’t worry. You’ll get your share,’ he said.

‘I know I will.’ I opened my car door and got in. ‘But it’s still my house as much as yours and I want to know what’s going on. Now I can tell my solicitor that you’ve got another woman living with you.’

He leaned on the car speaking through the driver’s window, but I drove away, pushing him off. I could see his face in my rear view mirror with that self-satisfied smirk. I would not give way to my feelings of anger, but I was more determined than ever to get this man out of my life.

~

True to my word, I informed my solicitor about the new partnership and he told Terry’s lawyer that I’d now be suing for adultery as well as unreasonable behaviour. Terry flatly denied the accusation, so my solicitor applied to Legal Aid for permission to engage a detective to watch the house for 24 hours in order to gather evidence of the existence of a new woman in Terry’s life. Our application was denied. My father offered to fund surveillance, wanting to do anything to get me free of Terry, but my solicitor advised us that if he paid for it, I’d lose my Legal Aid and would have to pay for the whole cost of the divorce.

Out of the blue, Terry offered through his solicitor £14,000 for my half of the house. Although this wasn’t anywhere near half the value of the property, my Dad and I agreed that this was the best offer I was likely to get. Although my solicitor wanted me to go for my full share,

I told him that I'd accept it if it meant the divorce would be finalised quickly.

As soon as Terry received my acceptance, he sent me a bill for the hiring of scaffolding and repainting the house's woodwork. The cheek of the man, expecting me to pay half of the bill, about 500 pounds, when I was struggling to make ends meet and provide for myself and my daughter.

In a panic, I asked my solicitor whether he could force me to pay. To rub salt in the wound, I received word of another sighting of Margot painting the windows and doors from a ladder.

Fortunately, my solicitor told me that I didn't have to pay a penny, since I'd accepted Terry's offer. After that, anything he did to the house was his problem. Still, there were a few hiccups along the way that made things more stressful than they needed to be. When we'd built the house, I took out credit in my name with the electric company to pay for the cooker. There were still four quarterly payment due and when I received the next bill, I was forced to tell the electric company that I couldn't afford to pay it. They informed me that they'd have to reclaim the cooker, something I was more than happy to agree to. How short-sighted of Terry to pull this stunt, costing him the cooker when we'd paid three quarters of the HP agreement.

Despite the trials and tribulations, the divorce was finalised and a decree nisi was granted on 10th March 1982, thus ending my marriage of eight years.

Chapter Twenty Five

My second marriage ended about 35 years ago now. Not a day goes by without my wishing that I could turn back the clock. I think about the way our selfish desire to taste life in the permissive society resulted in years of regret and misery. I will always feel guilty about the impact my actions had on my children's lives. My daughter tells me to move on and not carry this burden of guilt with me forever. In contrast, there were periods during his teenage years when my son could barely speak to me over the phone and he still has a great chip on his shoulder.

My daughter has had counselling to help her overcome her father's complete rejection of her. She tried for many years to have some kind of relationship with him, despite his coldness, but to no avail. She now says that at the age of forty three, she can move on and accept that she will never be a part of his life. She has two adorable boys who have never known their grandfather and he can't even be bothered to get their names right.

I wonder whether, if we'd known the consequences of our mad adventure all those years ago, would we still have carried on? Such was our fever and excitement when it all started that I fear nothing would have stopped us. We were all culpable and must all share the blame.

It is a truly fantastic story, stranger than fiction. I needed to write it down. Perhaps now I can exorcise some of my memories, assuage some of my guilt.

And how are we all now? Terry is still living with Margot, although I believe they never married. Rita and Robert have enjoyed over thirty years of marriage. My son married and had a son of his own but that marriage failed and now he has a new partner and a lovely little girl. My daughter faced the hardest task and has made the most progress, married with two sons.

As for me, I moved to France when I was fifty to live with my parents. My second marriage was my last and I don't have a regular partner. I am the proud owner of a lovely little house in an idyllic village situated on the banks of the Dordogne, just big enough for a pensioner of seventy.

I have been told by a number of clairvoyants over the years that the last section of my life will be the happiest and that I'd get married for a third time. I certainly hope the former is true, but I doubt very much whether I'll ever get married again.

"On verra" as we say in France!